Book 1

Marina Simcoe

Let Me Claim You
Seven Horny Sins

This book is a work of fiction. Names, characters, places, and incidents are a product of the author's imagination. Locales and public names are used for atmospheric purposes. Any resemblance to actual people, living or dead, or to businesses, companies, events, institutions, or locales is completely coincidental.
Spelling: English (American)
Editing by Cissell Ink
Proofreading by Owl Eyes Proofs & Edits
Cover image source Depositphotos.com
Cover design and illustrations by Marina Simcoe

No generative artificial intelligence (AI) was used in the writing or illustrating of this book. The author expressly prohibits any entity from using this publication to train AI technologies to generate text or pictures, including, without limitation, technologies capable of generating literary and artistic works.

Let Me Claim You contains graphic descriptions of intimacy and discussions on adult themes. Intended for mature readers.

Let Me Claim You

Seven Horny Sins
Book 1

Marina Simcoe

Madison

Pushing on the bag to compress the garbage inside it, I tied the ends, then heaved it out of the bin. It had been another busy day at the restaurant. If things continued moving this way, I might be able to move this place in the black this year.

Of course, with more customers, the amount of work increased too. It was nearly midnight already, but Claire and I had just finished cleaning the kitchen.

"You can go home," I said, dragging the bag to the back door. "I'll finish here and lock up."

"Are you sure?" Claire grabbed her purse from the counter but lingered, not rushing for the door as she usually would. As a single mother of a teenager, she always seemed to be in a hurry.

"There isn't much left to do," I assured her. "Just to take out the trash."

Taking the garbage out to the dumpster behind the restaurant was not in the job description of the Head Chef, or the

General Manager, or a few other positions I held as the owner of this place. Sam was supposed to do it, but his shift ended hours ago.

I really needed to hire more people. It'd be nice to have this place open for lunch and dinner seven days a week, including Mondays. But good employees weren't easy to find, and I had no time to look for them. Meanwhile, I ended up picking up the slack, not just cooking and running the kitchen, but also doing everything else that needed to be done.

Claire shifted her weight to her other foot, still not leaving. "Maddy, sweetie, can I borrow a hundred or two until my payday?" She put her palms together in a pleading gesture and sang, "Pleeease."

I set the bag on the floor by the back door and shoved my long, dark hair out of my face. My high bun had all but exploded during the vigorous cleaning.

"I'll give it back when I get paid," Claire promised. "You know I'm good for it."

She was. Mostly. Sometimes it'd take Claire far longer than "until the next paycheck" to repay it. Often, she simply forgot, and I never reminded her. Claire was a good friend and a loyal employee. The last thing I wanted was for money to stand between us.

"Sure. How much do you need?"

"One...um, no." She winced. "Make it *two* hundred. Josh needs new shoes. Again." She rolled her eyes. "I swear this kid grows too fast for me to keep up. And you know how teenagers are, he wouldn't wear just *any* shoes out there." She sighed. "I can't get away with buying secondhand for him anymore."

"Okay, but I don't have that much cash on me," I'd deposited what we had in the till that afternoon already. There wasn't that much to begin with as most transactions were cashless nowadays. "I'll stop at the bank on the way to work tomorrow, after I drive my mom to the dentist. Unless you want me to do a transfer?"

Claire beamed, grabbing me into a quick hug.

"Nope. Cash is good. Thanks." She rushed to the door. "Don't stay too long. Work isn't everything. You really should meet my neighbor. He's a long-haul truck driver, always on the road. You guys are made for each other. He'd fuck your brains out whenever he's in town, and let you work as much as you want the rest of the time."

If only I had any time to date even such a low-maintenance truck driver as Claire's neighbor. I spent every waking minute here. Even on Mondays, when the restaurant was closed, I had plenty of marketing and admin stuff to do every week. No one had "fucked my brains out" for over two years now.

Claire blew me a kiss before disappearing behind the swinging kitchen doors. "You're a lifesaver."

A lifesaver.

That was exactly what Sam had called me today when signing me up for a contribution to his second cousin's wedding gift.

"Can I put you down for five hundred?" he'd asked. "They don't have a lot of money but have this amazing honeymoon planned. It's like a once-in-a-lifetime thing."

Not that I had a lot of money, either. I'd spent every penny of my grandma's inheritance to lift this place off the ground. After two years of struggling to get our name out there, the restaurant had just started making some real money. The word about our tasty food had come out. There were lots of glowing reviews all over social media. We had waiting lines for each dinner service. Yet the more money came in, even more went out.

People often assumed I was "a woman of means" just because I owned a restaurant. In reality, there was a lot of debt to pay off before I could even think about moving out of my mom's basement one day.

But Sam, and Claire, and every one of the eleven people who worked for me were vitally important for my business. More than that, my employees were my friends, and I couldn't refuse helping friends, could I?

"It's just money." I brushed off the concerns and dragged the trash bag out into the dark alley behind the restaurant.

Squeezed between several high-rise buildings, the alley remained in the shadows even on a sunny day. At night, it was nearly pitch dark, especially since the light above the back door had gone out again. Or maybe some kids broke it. I sighed. Another thing to add to my "fix-it" list that already had plenty of things to fix both in the restaurant and back at home.

Thankfully, there was just enough light coming from the windows and from the street at the end of the alley for me to find my way to the dumpster.

A weird purple-green glow appeared from behind the dumpster as I approached, as if a bright neon sign was hidden there. People often dumped things here illegally. It wouldn't surprise me to find a broken storefront sign. Except that this one clearly wasn't broken. How was it even on?

"This world does not look the same as in Pandora's box," a deep, grumpy voice said suddenly, coming out of nowhere.

I squeaked in shock, dropping the trash bag, then turned around, searching for the source of the voice.

"And it smells," it complained with a strangled cough. "What the fuck is this stench?"

"The human world often stinks, but we don't have to stay here any longer," another voice replied, sounding just as low and eerie as the first one. "I got what I came here for. Let's head home."

"Wait, Avar. It's my first visit in decades, and all you let me see is this dark, stinky place? What is it, anyway? Where are we?"

The surreal voices echoed all around me, but I couldn't see their sources. There was no one in the alley, only darkness and the weird pulsing purple-green light coming from behind the dumpster.

Would they attack if I ran back to the restaurant?

Fear chilled my limbs. I grabbed the bag again. It wasn't much of a weapon, but it was all I had. Backing away in the darkness, I stepped on an empty soda can. It crushed under my foot, then rattled away as I jumped aside.

"Did you hear that?" the first voice asked.

I froze mid-step with my foot in the air.

"There is a human here." The second voice stated the obvious.

I'd been discovered. Now what?

Run?

What if they chased me?

And who the fuck were *they*, anyway?

"Who's there?" I shouted, trying to sound firm and assertive, and definitely not scared out of my wits.

"We should leave. You said it stinks here, anyway."

"Wait, let me see the human," the other voice insisted eagerly.

The green glow grew brighter, expanding from behind the dumpster and molding into an oblong shape.

My heart jumped into my throat.

Aliens!

What else could they be?

I stumbled back, tripped on a piece of trash, and fell on my ass, the bag landing on my lap.

"I have a security system here," I warned in a shaky voice,

using the garbage bag as a shield. "Leave now or I'll sound the alarm. The police will be here right away."

"A live human," a voice said breathlessly as the green light grew. "It's been a while since I saw one up close. Isn't she precious?"

The purple glow extended from behind the dumpster too. The mix of both proved blinding in the dark alley. I squinted, unable to see a thing.

"I know who she is," the other voice said with undisguised animosity. "Trust me, Invi, she isn't a good soul."

The accusation was unfair and simply outrageous.

"Hey!" A flash of indignity burned through my fear. "You don't even know me, asshole."

"See?" The voice said triumphantly, as if I had proven his point. "I may as well take her with me."

The purple glow grew brighter, flooding the ugly dumpster with a brilliant shimmer that was hard to look away from.

"Oh, hell, no!" I tried to scramble to my feet, but the garbage bag got in the way. I tripped over it in a hurry and fell on all fours. "No one is taking me anywhere."

"Her body won't survive her soul's journey, Avar, will it?" the other voice asked calmly.

"All humans die." The reply came serene and gentle, as if it wasn't a life-and-death situation they were discussing, *my* life and death. "She'll just get a chance to amend her ways a little sooner. And I will get a real human body for my collection."

"Is it *my* body you're talking about?" I jumped to my feet and swung the garbage bag at the approaching purple glow. "Stay away from me!"

The shimmer spread like ink through water.

Holding the bag in front of me, I backed all the way to the door until my butt slammed into it. I patted for the handle behind me. One push, and I'd be safe. They wouldn't break through the fireproof metal door, would they?

A thick, undulating tentacle stretched from inside the purple light, and my insides dropped with terror. A scream stuck in my throat.

"What a rare treasure her body will make," the ethereal voice growled with anticipation.

Then, the world went dark.

2

Madison

I woke up with a start, but my eyes refused to open right away. Thoughts rushed through my mind, urging my body to catch up and start moving.

There were so many things to do. I had to open the restaurant for lunch soon. Before that, I still needed to stop at the bank to get some cash for Claire, then pay for Sam's cousin's wedding present. I didn't even know the names of the couple. I should call Sam to ask.

Wasn't I supposed to drive Mom to the dentist this morning too?

My mind seemed fuzzy.

I had to force my eyes to open somehow, then go upstairs and see Mom. I hadn't left the house without saying goodbye to her since I was old enough to walk to the school bus on my own. Her "I love you" and a kiss on a cheek were like a good luck charm for me before starting my day.

"It's a nice body." A deep voice burst through the remnants of the sleepy fog lingering in my brain. "Pleasing to the eye."

"All bodies are essentially the same, Invi. Except that this one housed an undeserving soul," another deep voice replied somberly, triggering the memories of the dark alley and the glowing dumpster.

Had it been a dream?

If so, was I still dreaming?

I really needed to wake up already. The inability to move or even to open my eyes unnerved me.

"Where do you think her soul is now, Avar?" the voice I remembered as being addressed as Invi asked. "I didn't see it leave the body."

"In the human world, one can't see a soul. It becomes visible only here."

"Let's hope it doesn't linger in Purgatory and demand this body back. I'd most certainly want it back. It's a lovely one."

A grumpy sound followed the last comment. It appeared the one called Avar didn't appreciate Invi's admiration of "the body" they were talking about.

"What body was it?" I wondered, trying to force my mind to climb out of the fog and my limbs to start moving.

"Stop staring at it," Avar demanded.

"I'd love to. Sadly, I don't have another body to stare at instead, do I? Give me the transcendence potion. I'll go to the human world again and get one to stare at to my heart's content."

"I knew it was a mistake to bring you along," Avar groaned. "You never stop at 'just a look,' do you? Go home now, Invi. I have a lot of work to do, and I don't have much time. Physical bodies don't last long without a soul. This one will start rotting soon."

The one called Invi muttered something disgruntledly in response. Then, a weird swishing sound came, as if someone dragged something large over the floor.

Sensations returned slowly. The mattress felt weirdly firm, rock-hard actually. I stretched, my body finally responding to my mind. My feet hit something that crinkled and stank.

This wasn't my bed.

Alarm jolted me fully awake. My eyelids flew open at last.

The glass dome above me did not belong to my basement bedroom, neither did the view of the sunny skies beyond.

"What the..."

I rose on shaky elbows, squinting from the familiar purple glow. In the daylight, it proved far less blinding, allowing me to see the large figure inside it. A tall, bipedal creature with two pairs of horns stood just a couple of steps away from me. It turned, holding a long pane of glass in its hands and...in its tentacles.

"Aaaah!" I scrambled away as far as the long glass box I sat in would allow.

"Urgh!" the creature boomed, startled, and dropped the pane. The glass hit the stone floor and shattered into a million tiny pieces.

"You're alive?" The thing frowned.

"Do you want me dead?" With trembling fingers, I gripped the edges of the glass box I was in.

It was a long box, shaped suspiciously like a coffin. Kicking and slipping on the smooth glass, I desperately tried to get out. A black plastic bag at my feet burst open. Empty Styrofoam trays, foil wrappers, and other foul-smelling non-recyclables shot into the air like giant, disgusting confetti.

Tossing a leg over the edge of the glass box, I heaved myself out of it and fell. Or I would've fallen, if a thick glowing tentacle hadn't caught me and held me over the floor.

Panic exploded through me.

"Let me go!"

I pounded with both fists against the purple tentacle. It felt solid but looked transparent enough to see the floor and my feet through it.

What was this thing?

"Calm down, human," it rumbled, and I recognized one of the voices talking earlier. Avar, I remembered the name.

"Let go of me. Now!"

"And let you fall on the hard floor into the pile of broken glass?" Avar arched a bushy eyebrow, obviously unimpressed by my decision to leap out of the box.

A "pile of glass" was an exaggeration. The shards littered the floor in a thin layer. But it would still hurt if I fell. I stopped struggling, holding my hands away from the tentacle.

"Then set me down. I'll be fine. I'm wearing shoes."

All my clothes were still on, not just the shoes. Nothing was missing from my after-hours outfit for cleaning the kitchen: a pair of worn jeans, a red washed-out t-shirt, and old running shoes.

"If I set you down," he said, "promise me you won't do something stupid, like try to run. A physical body is too fragile. You must take care."

Running was exactly what I planned to do the moment my feet touched the ground.

But where would I run?

I glanced around. Where was I?

The room under the glass dome was round. Instead of walls, shelves and display cabinets surrounded it in a spiral that spread out and downwards, as if we were on top of a mountain enclosed in glass.

A lovely flowery scent filled the air through an arched opening in the glass that led out onto an open patio edged with bushes of the most purple lilacs I'd ever seen. The view of the ravine below the patio proved we really were high on top of a mountain. There were no exit signs. I had no idea where to run.

"Do you promise not to do anything that might damage your body?" Avar demanded.

"Fine. Yes. I promise."

It made sense. Ultimately, I had no desire to damage my body either.

The tentacle gently deposited me in the middle of the spiral design inlaid in the stone floor.

I took a step back and looked up at the creature, who was about twice as tall as me. It had a male torso with broad shoulders and thick, well-muscled arms. Two pairs of horns sprouted from his bald head. The two in the front were short and straight. The two on the back curled like the horns of a ram over his ears. Two tentacles extended from his sides right under his arms. I had to tilt my head back to see his face that was partially obscured by a long beard of undulating appendages that resembled thin snakes.

I backed away from the monster, glass crunching under my unsteady feet.

"Let me go, please," I asked softly. I didn't even care who he was or where we were, as long as I could make it home in one piece.

He leaned with his hip against the table and folded his arms over his chest. His long tentacles remained in motion, undulating around his thighs.

"I'm afraid I can't do that."

I remembered with a stab of fear that he'd spoken rather meanly about me with Invi. For some reason, this creature disliked me.

Was he punishing me for something?

"I've never seen you in my life before," I pleaded. "Trust me, I would've remembered if I had. If you hate me, there must be some mistake."

His broad chest rose with a deep breath.

"Hate is a very strong emotion. It would imply that I care, which I do not."

"You called me an *undeserving soul*. Why? Undeserving of *what?*"

"Of Invi's admiration."

"Who is Invi?"

"My brother." He shrugged a shoulder. "One of them."

"You have more?" The fact that this otherworldly creature had a family shocked me as much as that he existed at all.

"I have six brothers and seven sisters, if you must know."

No, I didn't need to know *that* or anything else about him as long as he would just deliver me back to where he took me from.

"You had no right to take me," I spat through my teeth, trying to hold back both anger and fear.

"I acquired you for my collection." He spread his tentacles in a wide gesture, encompassing the rows upon rows of shelves and display cases that cascaded down the mountain in a seemingly endless spiral.

"But I'm a person, not an exhibit."

"You can be both," he replied, unconcerned.

"It's not right. You can't keep a person the way you keep things. It's cruel, immoral, unethical, and—"

Propping his hands on his hips, he threw his head back and erupted into thunderous laughter.

"My dear human," he boomed. "I am a *mortal sin*—the very essence of immorality. In what world did you imagine I would behave *ethically?*" He shook his head at my naivety. "I'm the

Sin of Greed. I take what I like and never give anything back. Today, I got a chance to possess a mortal body. I saw yours. I took it. And now, it's mine."

"That's... That's kidnapping," I struggled for words, choked by terror. "It's a crime, you monster."

He squinted at me. "It's not like you've been living the life of a saint either, human."

The condescending note in his voice irked me. Anger overpowered the fear for a moment.

"My name is Madison." I hiked up my chin indignantly. "Maddy for friends, but not for *you*."

He huffed. "And mine is Avaricia, one of the mortal sins, or Avar for short. And I'm certainly not a 'monster,' even if your people made me look like one."

"*My* people? Who?"

A thought that someone from my restaurant might've been messing with him somehow rushed through my head. That would explain why he was angry with me. But *mortal sin?* What was that supposed to mean?

"By 'your people,' I meant humans in general," he explained, waving a tentacle in a vague gesture.

"Like...*all* humans?"

"Those who believe in sin and virtue, in heaven, and hell. Their beliefs created it all, me included." He spread his arms and tentacles wide. "Welcome to Purgatory, Madison."

"Purgatory?" I gasped. "Is that where we are?"

"A fitting place for someone like you." He wound one of his beard's long, slim appendages around his finger with a contemplative expression. "Though I really don't understand how your soul is still in your body."

"Did you expect it *not* to be in it?"

"That was my expectation. Yes."

"So, you tried to kill me?" People went to the purgatory *after* they died, didn't they? A wave of horror washed over me. "Am I dead?"

My stomach knitted into knots. I hiccupped, afraid I might throw up right there onto his glass strewn floor.

Avar cupped his chin, his "beard" spreading aside to accommodate the gesture.

"No, my dear. You are very much alive, in every sense of the word. Which is baffling, to tell you the truth."

"Are you..."

Are you planning to correct that? I was going to ask but didn't. Fear seized my throat at the thought that he might want to rectify the "mistake" and murder me. Besides being an otherworldly being, he was also bigger and probably stronger than me. It wouldn't take him much to end me.

A single word fluttered from my parted lips, instead.

"Why?"

"Why I find it baffling, you mean?"

"Why do you hate me so much?"

"Like I said, I don't hate you—" he stated evenly, but I'd had enough of that cool, indifferent attitude of his when my life as I knew it might be gone for good because of him.

"Of course you do. You want me dead!" I shrieked. "You clearly are disappointed that I didn't die when you stole me."

He seemed taken aback by my outburst.

"First of all, I don't steal, I *take,*" he corrected.

"What's the difference? Taking what doesn't belong to you is stealing."

"There are some fine nuances in your situation. All people die. Sooner or later, you'd end up here anyway."

"I would much rather it happened later than sooner."

"And speaking of stealing..." he continued, ignoring my

statement, "...you took your husband's research and dumped it in the garbage. Do you even understand the significance of his work? You might be the legal beneficiary of his possessions after his death, but that research didn't belong to you. It belonged to humanity. So, technically—"

I raised a hand, stopping him.

"What husband?"

"Fine, your *ex*-husband," he corrected. "You ruined his legacy by trying to destroy the results of his lifelong work. I saved it, and I will keep it. But because of you, it is now as good as lost to humankind forever."

"What *husband?*" I repeated, dumbfounded. "I don't have one. Not even an *ex*." I thrust both my ringless hands his way. "See? I'm not married. Never have been. I've no husband. No boyfriend. Heck, I haven't even been laid for years... Not that it's any of your business, of course."

His thick eyebrows moved closer together as he slid a quick once-over down my frame.

"Why not?"

"You want to know why my personal life is not your business?"

"No. I want to know why you haven't had sex. You are a grown woman in the prime of your current lifetime, aren't you? Why not?"

I nearly choked on my breath at his audacity.

"That's not what you have to worry about. You have clearly mistaken me for someone else. I never had a husband. I haven't stolen any research. The only thing I was throwing into the garbage that night was the actual garbage." I pointed at the mess in and around the glass box on the table. "You have to take me back. Please. I won't even demand an apology. Mistakes happen. Just bring me back to where you took me from, and I'll forget we ever met."

It'd be hard to forget someone like him, but once I'm back in my own bed safe and sound, I'd probably think of all of this as a dream.

He shifted his weight to another foot, looking slightly uncomfortable.

"Sadly, I can't do it. If you really aren't the ex-wife of Professor Lozhkin, I apologize for bringing you here. I really thought you came back to that waste container to toss more of his belongings out."

"I said I don't need your apologies. Just take me back."

"Like I said, I can't do it. I can't give. I only take."

My heart dropped.

"What do you mean? How hard would it be to bring me back and pretend none of this ever happened?"

"It's not the difficulty of traveling between our worlds that's stopping me, Madison. Though the travel itself isn't simple, either. It's the act of giving. I'm incapable of it. In the millennia of my existence, I have never returned a single thing I took."

"It's never too late to start," I suggested, holding on to hope with all I had.

"You don't understand, my dear. My very nature is to take. Giving would kill me."

"But giving is a beautiful thing—"

"I said it will not happen!" His voice thundered so loudly, it was a shock that the glass dome didn't shatter. Bright red flashed through his purple glow. His beard undulated wildly, spreading aside.

I backed away. My butt hit a display cabinet behind me.

"Careful!" He stretched both his arms and his tentacles toward me and the cabinet. "These things are irreplaceable."

Was I supposed to become one of his "things" now? I glanced at the glass box he prepped on the table.

"You want to put me in there?" I whimpered, pressing my back to the flimsy cabinet. "Is that what you have it ready for?"

"Well, a physical body is a highly perishable thing. I had to preserve it. Now that you happened to be alive, however..." He gave me a long, assessing look.

"You want to kill me?" I finished for him.

"Actually, no..." he said as if thinking out loud. "I believe I far prefer you alive. Around here, a live human is just as rare as a physical body but can also be far more amusing."

He took a step toward me, and I cowered under the curio cabinet with some shiny stones assembled in elaborate metal frames.

"You find my distress amusing?" Unwelcome tears blurred my vision, burning my eyes.

He paused, taking in my shivering body and my flushed face.

"No, my dear, your distress brings me no joy whatsoever. In fact, I find seeing you like this highly unpleasant." He crouched down to my level. "There is no need to fear death, Madison," he spoke kindly, as if explaining to a child. "Death is simply a passage from one world to another. Your soul is immortal. But if you're fond of the body you're currently in, you can keep it. I promise as long as you're with me, no one will separate you from it until its natural deterioration."

That proved oddly reassuring. He certainly seemed big and powerful enough to stop anyone from harming me. As long as he didn't harm me himself, of course.

A tentacle reached for me, and I shrank back from it. He immediately jerked away the undulating appendage.

"All right, I won't touch you against your will either," he assured me. "I take care of what's mine. I'll keep you safe. Now, will you relax a little and stop looking like a kicked puppy? It makes me extremely uncomfortable to see you miserable like that." He made a face as if he'd bitten into a lemon. "Since you seem to be attached to that body of yours, you can keep it for as long as it'll hold you. I won't put it on display until after your soul departs it." He looked pleased with himself. I would bet my restaurant on it, he saw it as a generous offer.

"What if I live for another sixty years or more?" I asked carefully. At my thirty-two, it was a reasonable lifespan to expect.

"Then you'll live here for sixty years or more," he replied casually.

Chilling dread gripped my insides. My limbs shook. But cowering under the cabinet would not get me home.

I fisted my hands, silently gathering my resolve. Since he wouldn't bring me back, I'd have to do it on my own. If I ever wanted to see my friends, my mom, and my restaurant ever again, I had to stay strong. I had to think. I needed to learn more about this place to find a way out of here.

"Let's figure out a suitable accommodation for you meanwhile." Avar straightened to his full height. The broken glass crunched under his feet. He lifted a foot and scowled at the shards. The mess clearly displeased him, but the glass didn't cut him. He didn't seem to be in pain. There was no blood on the floor, either. Could he even bleed?

Avar obviously wasn't human. Glowing and semi-transparent, he didn't even seem real. If I squinted, I could see the shelves behind him *through* him. Yet he wasn't an incorporeal ghost. His large, tall shape was solid. I felt it when he held me with his tentacle.

He wore not a stitch of clothing, and his crotch area was Ken-doll smooth. At least in the most obvious visual sense, Avar wasn't a he or a she.

A mortal sin?

How could that be true?

He bent over the floor and made a sweeping gesture in the air with his open palms. The glass shards slid along the floor, shifting in a circle, then gathering into a pile. Avar waved his hands in the air, and the shards thinned, then melted like ice in hot air. Unlike ice, however, they didn't leave a puddle on the floor. They just disappeared without a trace.

"Where did the glass go?" I blinked, dumbfounded.

Avar flicked a wrist. "Into the ether."

"Ether?"

"Exactly." He nodded. "Everything here comes from and returns to the ether."

"I did not know that."

"Well, now you do."

Whether I wanted to or not, I needed to know more about this place and this being since both my life and freedom were in his hands and...well, in his tentacles too.

"Who is your brother? The one who was here before?" I asked as he stared at the garbage strewn over the table. "The one you called Invi?"

He jerked his head my way, his beard's appendages flaring to the sides to resemble a chrysanthemum for a moment.

"You heard him here?"

"Yes. Both here and back at the dumpster." Maybe I could convince Invi to take me back since Avar refused?

"Invidia is the Sin of Envy..." Avar heaved a sigh. "He went back home now, and he'd better stay there. I don't trust him around my collection. That scoundrel always wants what others have."

He glared at the valley outside the patio, in the direction where I suspected Invi's home must be.

"It's understandable," I said. "As the Sin of Envy, it'd be in his nature, I suppose."

"Is that so?" Avar squinted at me. "How are you so very understanding about his nature, but so disapproving of mine? If you excuse *him* for being envious, why can't you understand *me* holding on to my possessions?"

It was the "possession" part that aggravated me the most. How could he expect me to be forgiving about treating me as such?

"Why does it matter how I feel about you?" I snapped. "You said you don't care, anyway."

"I *shouldn't* care." He stomped around, moving the items on the shelves and adjusting the cabinets around us. Stopping abruptly in front of me, he folded his arms on his chest and propped his tentacles on his hips. "I shouldn't care, but I do. I want to derive pleasure from every exhibit in my collection. It irritates me to know that you dislike me."

"You really need me to like you?" I asked incredulously.

Did the Sin of Greed crave affection?

He paused in concentration, as if listening to his own desires.

"I would prefer it if you did. Yes," he confessed.

I folded my arms over my chest, too, mimicking his stance as much as I could without the tentacles.

"To be liked, people usually do nice things for each other. Being kind helps. What have you done for me? You snatched me away from the people and places I hold dear. You told me I'm to stay here until the day I die."

"I said 'for as long as your body will hold you,'" he corrected. "Your body is mine, but your soul is free to go as it pleases. For some reason, however, it chooses to cling to this body."

"*For some reason?* Do you not understand why people don't want to die?"

"I thought I explained it clearly that death is simply a switching point in a soul's journey. A soul doesn't cease to exist by vacating a body." He slid an assessing gaze down my frame, tilting his head. "I have to admit it is actually a very nice body. I can see how you'd be reluctant to part with it."

There was that interest in his eyes again as when I'd mentioned I hadn't had sex for some time. It made my skin tingle in response in a way I oddly did not find unpleasant.

As unusual as Avar looked, there was as much mesmerizing in his purple shimmer as there was terrifying in his giant shape. The longer I stared at him, the more drawn in I felt, and the stronger the fear pulsed in my chest. Like I wished to take a step off a cliff, even knowing that the fall would kill me.

"What exactly do you need my body for?" I asked. "Are you sure it's just to display it?"

Despite having nothing between his legs, Avar didn't appear to be indifferent to sex. And now, I really didn't know how to take his desire to claim my body *without* the soul.

"What else could there be?" He blinked innocently.

I squinted at the trash in the glass box.

"Why did you take the garbage bag too?"

He followed my eyes with his, then rubbed the back of his neck uncertainly.

"It looked like it belonged with you."

"Belonged with me." I stared at him. "Kind of like a Barbie accessory?"

"Barbie?" He looked confused for a moment, then his beard parted with a smile. "You mean the doll?"

"You know about the Barbie doll?"

Should I be shocked? After all, we met in my world. He spoke the language I understood and claimed to be the embodiment of human beliefs. It wouldn't be much of a stretch to imagine he was familiar with many human cultures as well, and Barbie was well known pretty much all over the globe.

"As much as I despise many of the actions of humans that I've witnessed over my existence," he explained, "I go to your world from time to time to retrieve items for my collection. Also, on our last birthday celebration, Mother gifted us a magical vision box that helps learn the most current things about your world. Yes, I know about Barbie. Come to think of it..." He scratched his chin. "Your body would've looked like a doll in that glass box, with or without the garbage bag accessory."

"And would you have just looked at it? Nothing else?"

He glanced at me in question, then understanding spread across his face.

"Are you implying that my intentions were to violate a lifeless body? Madison, that's simply disgusting," he scolded.

A blush warmed my face. "In my defense, you did describe yourself as the very essence of immorality."

"Immorality is not the same as grossness or vulgarity. Like most people and all my brothers, I enjoy things that bring pleasure, including sex. But like everyone else around here, I engage in such activities exclusively with souls. A body-less soul is a far more appropriate sex partner than a soulless body." A shudder ran through his massive frame as he muttered to himself, "Sex with a motionless body? It'd be like humping a pile of discarded clothes."

I tried to process all the things he'd just said.

"Are you saying that souls have sex?"

"Of course they do. I mean they *can* if they want to, here in Purgatory and in any of the paradises where sex is possible."

"Is there more than one paradise?"

"Thousands of them." He nodded. "Humans collectively possess a boundless imagination."

"And some of those places allow sex?"

"Many of them do. Generally, when crossing into another world, people want to leave their sufferings behind, but not their pleasures. However, it all depends on every soul's beliefs of course. Would you prefer to be in a paradise without sex?"

"I would really prefer to be back on Earth."

He squinted at me again.

"That's strange. Souls usually dislike returning to the human world. But then again," he pondered, "many dislike waiting in Purgatory too. Souls are restless creatures who often prefer to be on the way to some place they think is better. Not all paradises are as great as they think, you know. Some of them are pretty boring, I've heard."

"How do souls have sex without a body? Like...how do *you*

have sex?" I tried very hard not to stare at his crotch, despite its perfectly decent smooth appearance. "You're a spirit, aren't you?"

"I'm an incorporeal entity," he clarified with pride. "I don't need a physical body. I have a presence without it."

"But doesn't one need a body in order to have sex?" I insisted.

I wondered how we even came to this point in our conversation, but now I needed to know the answer.

"In order to procreate, yes, having a physical body is important," he said. "However, sex is so much more than that. True pleasure is felt in your soul, and pleasure is the essence of a sin's existence. Of course, I can have sex. After all, the Sin of Lust is one of my brothers." He tugged at his beard in contemplation. "I don't think I'm going to let you meet him, though. In fact, there is no need for you to meet any of my brothers at all. I don't share what's mine."

"But I'm not yours," I said quickly, anxious to set things straight between us. "I don't know what laws you have here, but if human beliefs created your Purgatory, then my soul is supposed to be free. That is the basis of every belief I know. And since my soul is free, you can't have it. And because it's in this body, you can't have sex with it either. You promised I could keep it, and I don't want you to have sex with it."

"You don't?" He looked disappointed. "Why not? I mean, sex wasn't my intention when I took your body. But now that your soul is staying in it, why not? Why deprive yourself of the pleasure I could give you?"

"Free will," I blurted out the first thing that came to mind. "I don't want to have sex with you. Ever. You stole me from my world. You brought me here without my permission. Why do you even think I'd want to have anything to do with you at all?"

He stretched his neck with a grunt, then started picking up

the garbage from the glass box on the table and stuffing it into the ripped bag. He didn't use his "ether magic" to dispose of it, looking too distracted by his thoughts. I wondered if he forgot that he even possessed it.

"Fair enough," he finally agreed, to my utter surprise. "No sex it is, then."

3

Madison

While Avar took away the trash and the glass box, I was left unsupervised. I immediately searched around the room, looking for the way out. Avar might be greed personified, unable to let go, but I had things to do back home. I wasn't going to sit here for decades, just waiting for my soul to move on.

There was only one path out from the room on the top of the mountain, and I followed it down the mountainside. The path curved and turned, bypassing valleys and ridges in the rock. Occasionally, it widened into a platform. Other times, it narrowed to a bridge over a gorge.

Shelves and cabinets lined the path on both sides, displaying the items in the Sin of Greed's collection. Some looked like rocks or minerals. Others resembled jewelry or dishes. There were books and scrolls of all sizes, jars filled with weird liquids, and dried, creepy, gnarly things that I tried not to look at too closely.

A part of me wished to stop and examine some of the items in detail. I almost wished Avar was here to tell me more about his exhibits. But if I lingered, I risked eventually becoming an exhibit myself, with my dead body sealed into a glass box and displayed somewhere along this path too.

Crossing a bridge over a bubbly creek running deep below, I realized I was both torturously thirsty and in dire need of a bathroom. I looked for anything resembling a bathroom, fearing that there might not be one at all.

Did deadly sins pee?

Probably not, since Avar seemed to be missing the organ to perform that function.

I came upon a cave in the wall. It was dark inside, but the need for a bathroom became unbearable, urging me to explore. Sadly, I found no toilet here either. As far as I could see, the cave was filled with things that Avar probably hadn't had the time to put on display yet.

Rolls of hides, fabrics, and rugs had been leaned against the smoothly polished walls of the spacious cave. Trunks, boxes, and bags piled up, filled with books, carvings, and artifacts. Crates with dishes and scrolls crowded the floor, leaving only a narrow path for me to maneuver around.

"The Sin of Greed is an honest-to-God hoarder," I muttered to myself.

The call of nature grew increasingly more intense. Sadly, Avar's mountain didn't appear to have any bathroom at all.

Pressing my legs together in desperation, I eyed a wide red-and-black vase by the wall.

What would be worse? Using the vase that looked antique, expensive, and possibly cursed as a chamber pot? Or peeing in my pants?

"What are you doing here?" a deep voice boomed behind

me, nearly making the decision for me. Startled, I almost peed my pants.

"Avar?" I turned around to face the beast of a sin.

His massive shape filled the entrance. Blocking the outside light, he illuminated the dark cave with his own glow.

My breath hitched at the sight of him. It was impossible not to stare as he hovered in the entrance, his horns almost touching the high ceiling, his wide shoulders blocking the way, his tentacles spreading along the wall on each side of him. Human imagination truly had no bounds to come up with a creature like that.

"Why are you in here?" he demanded. "I was looking for you up at the top where I left you."

"Was I expected to stay put, like a good 'exhibit?'" A hefty dose of sarcasm spiced my reply. "If so, you should know that it doesn't work for live humans. Unlike objects or dead bodies, we tend to move around."

He narrowed his eyes at me. "I have plenty of means to restrain you."

Apprehension trickled down my spine, making me bite my tongue this time.

"What would you prefer?" he inquired casually. "A cage, a leash, or a ball with a chain around your leg?"

"How about a word?" Somehow, I managed to sound calm.

"A word?" He looked confused.

"Yes. Next time, just tell me where you expect me to be, and I may listen if you ask nicely."

"Hmh." He moved back his shoulders, pondering my words.

"Meanwhile..." I cleared my throat. "Do you happen to have a toilet around here?"

"What kind of a toilet?"

"The kind I could pee in."

"Pee?"

As I had feared, he was clueless on the topic.

"Humans pee," I explained. "And...do other things in bathrooms."

"Oh, a bathroom!" He perked up. "You need to use a bathroom."

He headed to the closest wall with enthusiasm, then shoved some crates and trunks out of the way.

I followed him. "You know, if you intend to keep me around, there are many more things I'll need. For one, I'm very thirsty."

He gave me a glance over his shoulder. "So, you need to drink water *and* expel it at the same time?"

I nodded. "Funny, isn't it? Humans really are a nuisance when you think about it. Physical bodies need so much care. I'll have to eat and drink several times a day, and I tend to get unbearably cranky when I skip a meal. I'll need a bathroom close by, a bed to sleep in, clothes, shoes, soaps, showers, hairbrushes, toothpaste, nail clippers... I'm way too high maintenance, compared to the other things in your collection." I sighed sympathetically. "It'd really be so much easier for you to just take me back."

His beard shifted, its long slim appendages arranging into a pattern that betrayed a smile underneath.

"Clever little human, aren't you? Do you really think a small inconvenience will be enough for me to give you up?"

Sadly, an ancient being proved not that easily fooled.

"I'll make you a bathroom," he promised.

He splayed a hand on the wall of the cave. Ripples ran from his fingers, making the hard, solid rock look like it was liquid. When he pushed, the rock gave in. He stepped forward, and the mountain retreated from around him, forming a cave.

"Wow..." I exhaled, poking a finger into the remaining wall that was as hard as ever. "How did you do it?"

He shrugged. "It's *my* mountain. I can do whatever I want with it."

Inside the newly formed cave, the rock rose in the middle of the floor, forming a toilet bowl.

"And there it is." Avar pointed at it proudly. "A bathroom with a toilet." He ran the tip of his right tentacle around the bowl, forming a ring of carved designs on the outside.

"What's the function of that?" I pointed at the carvings.

He tilted his head, inspecting his handy work. "It's prettier this way, don't you think?"

The toilet really looked stunning, like a piece of art carved from red and gray granite. I peeked inside it. There was a shallow opening in the middle of the bowl, but no water and obviously no plumbing.

"Sadly, this won't work," I said.

"Why not?"

"There is no way to flush it. Where is the...uhm, *waste* supposed to go?"

He huffed a deep laugh. "In the ether, my sweet heart. Don't you worry, it will all go in the ether."

"How convenient," I noted, unbuttoning my jeans.

Beggars couldn't be choosers. I had to go so badly. Just a minute ago, I contemplated desecrating a vase from his collection. At least this one, Avar claimed, was a toilet.

I turned around, ready to sit on it, and froze.

Avar remained at the entrance to the new cave. Leaning against the wall, his arms folded across his chest, he looked expectant and ready for a show.

"What are you doing?" I yanked my pants back up.

"I've never seen anyone using a toilet before," he explained excitedly. "In the viewing box that Mother gave us, humans talk about going to the bathroom sometimes. They show toilets too. But they never actually use them."

"Yeah... Well, I'm not going to use it with you watching, either."

"Why not?"

"Because people don't pee in front of other people if they can help it. You have to leave."

He grunted, looking disappointed.

"Fine." He turned around and stomped away.

Relieved, I finally used the toilet. When I was done, the bowl remained as clean and dry as before I started.

"Ether," I marveled. "How cool is that?"

When I exited the bathroom, Avar was nowhere to be found.

"Avar?"

"Over here!" his deep voice echoed from around the bend of the path.

I found him in another cave just around the corner. This one was shallow, more like a niche in the mountainside than a cave. The path ran under it with a set of stairs leading up to the platform in front of the cave with a gorgeous view of the valley below through the glass dome over the mountain.

"This is stunning..." I admired the emerald valley flooded with golden sunlight.

"You like it?" Avar seemed pleased. He stood over a wide bed inside the cave. "Will this be an acceptable place for you to sleep?"

Puffy comforters and furs piled on top of a rock-bed platform.

"Did you just make it? All of it?" I asked.

"The cave and the platform, yes. But the bedding is from my collection. Griffin fur and banshee feathers make for the most comfortable sleep."

"Are you saying that griffins and banshees are real?"

"In some worlds, they are. They used to be found in your world too. But that was a very long time ago, long before they even started calling me a mortal sin."

That brought another question to mind.

"How old are you, exactly?"

"Exactly?" He chuckled. "Greed is as old as humanity itself. Do you want to know how long it's been since I got a name? Or how long I've been called a sin?"

I considered his words for a moment.

"It doesn't really matter, does it?" His age made no difference in my situation. "Either way, you're incomprehensibly old, right?"

"Right." He smiled. "Ancient."

I lowered my butt onto the edge of the bed, sinking into the cushy bedding. It felt comfy and so inviting. My eyelids dropped as a warm wave of sleepiness washed over me.

"I'll move the bathroom closer..." Avar's voice drifted to me through the haze of exhaustion, "...and divert the mountain creek to it, so you'll always have access to water. For food, I'll have to talk to Gul. Also, Sup has enough clothes to dress an army, which would make it the best-dressed army across all words too."

"Who are Gul and Sup? More of your brothers?" I guessed.

"Right. Gula, the Sin of Gluttony, and Superbia, the Sin of Pride. For a while there, you humans loved using Latin to name everything."

"We sure did," I agreed, struggling to keep my eyes open. Maybe I could take a quick nap? Just to rest my eyes for a minute or two, before continuing to search for a way to escape?

"Chances are, you won't see any of my family. I loathe anyone poking their noses into my business. But when I need help, my brothers are the first ones I go to. My sisters are useless."

"Oh, right, you have sisters, too, and a mom. Where are they?"

"Our mother is rarely around." He crouched by the bed, and I realized I'd tilted sideways at some point and now rested my cheek on the softest pillow ever. "You need some rest. You look tired."

"Do mortal sins ever rest?" I asked.

"Of course we do. But some of us rest more than others. Just ask my brother Ace." He chuckled.

"Ace must be Sloth?" I murmured, letting my eyelids drop.

"That's right. Acedia, the Sin of Sloth." He pulled a soft fur blanket over me.

Sleep hovered close, and I had no strength to resist it. One thought wouldn't let me rest, however.

I popped my eyes open.

"Avar?"

He was on his way out already. "I'll get you some water. You said you were thirsty."

"I am but... Can I ask you for a favor, please?"

He seemed accommodating right now, and I had to use the moment. Who knew what mood he might be in next?

His brow furrowed in a frown, however.

"If it's about letting you go—" he started, his voice dipping in warning.

"No. It's not about that." He'd made it clear he wouldn't release me. If I wanted to go back, I had to find my own way. "It's about my life back home. Is there a way to let my mom and my friends know what happened to me? Can I send them a message?"

He tilted his head. "A message from beyond the grave?"

I fought a shiver of dread at his words. "But I haven't died.

There'd be no dead body, no note, nothing for the people who love me to have closure."

"Are there many of those who loved you?"

"Well, I have a restaurant with eleven employees. They need to know why I didn't show up for work. And my mom..." I swallowed hard, struggling to hold it together. "I'm the only family she has. It'll kill her not knowing."

He moved his jaw, scratching his chin.

"Please," I begged. "I can write a quick note if there is any way for you to deliver it. A note wouldn't be for you, so it's not like you'd be giving up your possession, right? It'd be for my mom to tell her that I'm well."

"Are you planning to tell her the truth? How do you envision it? Do you really believe it would make your mother feel better to learn that her daughter is in Purgatory for the rest of her current lifetime?"

A note like that would probably make her think that I didn't just disappear without a trace but also completely lost my mind in the process.

I released a heavy sigh, disheartened.

"What is the best thing to do here, then?"

With a grant, Avar left my little cave of glass and rock, and I remained sitting in bed, racked by the worry strong enough to overpower my exhaustion.

He returned just a few moments later and handed me a glass of water.

"Here." He placed an antique writing desk by the wall and a chair that he carried in his tentacles.

I gulped the water, watching him open the hatch of the desk and arrange a quill, ink, and a sheet of paper on the writing surface.

"Write the note as your last will and testament," he said.

"Settle your affairs, because you're not returning to that life ever again."

I drew in a shaky breath, as a heavy feeling of gloom settled over me.

"We'll see about that," I said in my head, holding on to hope and defiance.

"Will you deliver it?" I asked.

"That's the least I can do," he muttered into his beard.

4

Madison

I woke up to the view of a gorgeous sunset in the valley. After admiring the vivid colors for a little while, however, I realized the sun was climbing up, not setting down. It was early morning already. I slept through the remainder of yesterday and through the entire night.

A waterfall trickled gently in the creek that Avar had diverted to run through my bathroom. The sound was soothing, but not enough to calm my anxiety. I'd written my will last night. Avar delivered it to my mother's address. She would get it today, and I could only imagine what she'd think.

Settling my business affairs and even saying a vague goodbye in a legal paper was not the same as giving someone a parting hug and kiss. I would never see my mom again, and all because of the whim of an otherworldly entity incapable of letting anything or anyone go.

How could I live with that? I had to find a way to get out of here.

As I was getting ready to leave my cave, the mountain trembled slightly, making me pause.

Was it an earthquake?

I grabbed on to the nearest wall for balance and suddenly wished Avar was here. His large form and over-the-top confidence would give me some reassurance.

Unlike an earthquake, though, it wasn't just the ground that shook. The air around me appeared to ripple too. Even the glass dome appeared to waver like a mist.

When it all stilled again, voices came from below. The deep, growly one I immediately recognized as Avar's. The other voice sounded lighter and far more melodious.

"Can I meet her?" the pretty voice implored. "Please?"

"No," Avar cut off. "Thanks for the food and the dress. Now, bye."

I rushed down the path that led me into an open space at the foot of the mountain. An arch of golden filigree marked the entrance into Avar's domain of rock, glass, and ancient treasures.

A lone figure stood inside the arch. The semi-transparent shape of our visitor glowed like Avar's. Unlike him, however, this glow was of shimmering gold, not purple. By the wide hips and voluptuous breasts, I wondered if the spirit was a female, if spirits had a gender.

The golden person grinned, tilting her head to see me behind Avar's massive body towering over us. "Is that her?"

Avar turned around, balancing a covered tray in one of his tentacles and a long piece of bright orange fabric in the other.

"Why are you here?" he demanded, finding me standing behind him.

"The place shook," I said. "Then I heard voices. What's going on?"

He positioned himself solidly between me and the

newcomer, as if trying to shield me from her view. It accomplished little, since I could still see the person's glowing outline through his form, and she probably could see me too.

"The mountain doesn't like invasions," Avar explained, scowling in the direction of the golden spirit. "And neither do I."

"I'm here to do you a favor," the spirit protested. "You asked for food." She snatched both the tray and the cloth from him, then turned to me. "Breakfast, courtesy of Gul, my roommate. And a dress from his brother, Sup. If you like them, I'll bring more of both."

I took a deep breath of the mouth-watering aroma that wafted from the tray in her hands, trying and failing to figure out what dish was under the lid.

"It smells delicious." My stomach growled with anticipation. I hadn't eaten in what seemed like forever. "Thank you. You have no idea how happy I am to see you. I'm starving. I'm Madison, by the way." I stepped toward her, offering her my hand.

Avar's tentacles sprang around me but didn't touch me or hold me back, just hovering around me in a protective semi-circle.

"Hi, Madison." The spirit gave my hand a firm shake, holding the tray in her other hand. "It's so nice to meet you. What part of the world did you come from? Mediterranean? Latin America?" She slid her gaze over my long dark hair and light-brown skin, then paused on my tattered jeans and worn t-shirt with *I heart cats* written on it in English. "England? North America, maybe?" She waved a hand before I could answer. "Not that it matters. We're all just souls here, all speaking the same language, as you might've noticed by now. I'm E, by the way."

"E? Is that your name? Just one letter?"

"Souls don't have names," Avar dismissed.

E pouted in his direction. "But what if I feel like having one?" She then turned to me again. "I can't remember what they called me back when I had a body. But I have a feeling that most of my names in my past lives started with E."

"You've lived more than one lifetime?"

"Mhm." She nodded. "Fourteen to be precise."

"Wow. So many? That's more than a cat has. And you don't remember a single name?"

"For souls, names aren't important. What matters are our experiences during all the different lives and what we learn from them."

"So...right now, you're dead?"

She giggled. "Of course not. Souls don't die. I'm just, um... well, between bodies at the moment." She slid her hand up my forearm, prodding and squeezing. "It's so bizarre to see a real body in Purgatory."

I didn't mind her touching. I imagined I'd be even more amazed if I saw a disembodied spirit back in my world.

Avar cleared his throat, hands propped on his hips, his tentacles undulating irritably.

"Well, you've seen her. Now goodbye, E." He gestured toward the exit.

"No. Stay," I said quickly. "Please, can she have breakfast with me?"

I wasn't ready to let her go. I had so many questions. And the talkative, outgoing E seemed to be just the right person to answer them all.

"I'll gladly join you," she chirped, sashaying past Avar, who appeared to have gone speechless at her audacity.

"Who said she can stay?" He finally found his voice.

"Just for a little while, please?" I pressed my palms together in a pleading gesture. "I'd love to have company for breakfast. It sucks to eat alone."

His beard moved as he mulled over my request, looking tormented. On one hand, he clearly disliked the invasion of his space. On the other hand, he seemed committed to keeping me happy, probably out of guilt for snatching me away from the only life I could remember.

E smiled at him sweetly. "I promise not to touch any of your things."

"You'd better," he grumped, then waved along the path. "You can go up to Madison's room. But you can stay here only for as long as it takes her to eat breakfast."

That was better than nothing.

"Thanks." I hurried away before he might change his mind. "Do you want me to take the tray?" I asked E.

"I'm fine." She waved me off, easily carrying the large thing in one hand.

"It's not too far," I assure her. "This mountain looks huge, but it doesn't take that long to get around."

"It's because the path moves."

"It does?" I stopped and stared at the smooth rocks under my feet.

There was no discernible movement, but when I raised my head, the cabinet I'd stopped next to was now way behind us.

"I never noticed." I headed forward again. "Have you been here before?"

E nodded. "A few times. Between my past lives. But I'm mostly staying with Gul this time. It's more fun at his place. He also really knows how to cook. Wait until you try this." She tipped her chin at the tray in her hand.

"Souls don't need to eat, do they?"

"No. I don't need food, but I do enjoy it. Isn't it great? You can eat all you want, and it doesn't matter how you look."

Like Avar, E had not a stitch of clothing on her, but I wouldn't call her naked. Her shape lacked the details of a physical body—like fine hair on her arms or pores on her skin. Her breasts had no nipples, and the area between her legs was also perfectly smooth. Gathered into a long, high ponytail, her hair streamed down her back in a mass that had no definition of individual strands.

"You're staring." Her voice snapped me out of my contemplation.

"I am," I admitted. "Sorry. It's just that I've never seen a soul without a body before."

She cocked her hip. "So, what do you think?"

"It's...interesting. Is that how we all look inside?"

She laughed. "Oh God, no. Wouldn't that be the most boring sight in the afterlife? The visible shape of a soul bears no meaning. It's the inner substance that matters. The shape is easy enough to change." Balancing the tray away from her, E gestured down her torso. "Look."

Suddenly, her full breasts shrank, and her curvy hips narrowed, giving her a slimmer appearance. But E's transformation didn't stop there. The hair on her head shortened. Instead, a full beard sprang from her chin and cheeks. Her shoulders widened; her chest molded into a pair of well-defined pectoral muscles.

"I can go all the way if you want." She laughed. Her voice remained completely unchanged, despite the dramatic visual transformation. A huge dick suddenly sprouted between her now very muscular thighs. It grew longer and thicker, reaching grotesque size and proportions, until its bulbous head dangled somewhere way past her knees. "Every guy's dream, isn't it?" She winked at me. "Or is it every girl's?"

"Um...not to that extent. Please," I laughed with her. "At least, not for me."

With a relieved "oomph" E released a breath, snapping back into her previous shape. The beard and the giant penis were now gone.

"Oh, this feels much better," she said. "A firmly defined appearance is an attribute of a physical body. A soul can be anything it wants. But I feel more comfortable in this shape right now. Probably because I was a woman in my most recent life. Sometimes, it takes a while to...you know, *decompress* from your last physical form once you leave the constraints of a body."

"Have you been a man in some of your past fourteen lives too?"

She nodded. "A man, a woman, and everything in between and outside of that. I've been around long enough to try it all, or almost all, I think."

It was all so fascinating, I could chat with E forever. But I had to focus and stay on topic if I ever wanted to escape Purgatory.

"How do you travel to and from here?"

Her smooth forehead creased with a frown. "Well, the travel has never been up to me. The Higher Judgment evaluates all the deeds of the soul during its lifetime, then decides what to do with it next."

"And what are the options?"

"Not many. If deemed worthy, the soul is sent to the paradise of its choosing. Those who have really fucked up end up in hell. And some of us who supposedly need more 'learning,'" she made a quotation sign with the hand not holding the tray, "keep getting sent back to Earth over and over again." She rolled her eyes. "It gets fucking exhausting, to be honest."

We turned off the path and up the stairs to my platform.

"Well, here's my room." I led E under the glass dome, took

the dress from her and laid it onto the bed as she set the tray on the round table in the middle of my living space.

"This is cute." She took a twirl around before lifting the lid off the tray. "Dig in since you're starving."

The appetizing aroma intensified. My stomach cramped, and I almost tripped on my way to the table.

"God, it smells so good."

E grinned. "See why I'm staying with a mortal sin instead of getting a cute little place of my own in town?"

"What town?" I gaped at her.

"Purgatory, of course."

"Is it an actual town?"

She nodded and picked up what looked like a dumpling from the platter on the tray. "A town for us poor souls to hang around until the Higher Judgment about our future is made."

I looked at the platter laden with all possible kinds of food, from pierogis, to sushi, to things I'd never seen before. Grabbing something that looked like a steamed bun, I bit into it and moaned in pleasure.

"So good."

E gave me a knowing look. "Told you." She finished her dumpling and took another one. "Coffee?" she asked around a mouthful while picking up a small silver carafe with steam curling out of its curved spout.

"Please." I sat at the table and pulled the platter closer.

The more I ate, the bigger my appetite grew.

"Something I don't understand," I said, taking a cup of coffee from E. "I'm not an expert, but if I remember correctly, the purpose of Purgatory is to cleanse us of our sins, right? How is living with one of them supposed to help you with that?"

E stuffed an éclair into her mouth, speaking around it as she ate.

"If a pleasure-less paradise is your thing, by all means, cleanse and go. That's not what I want, though."

"What do you want?"

"I want to have fun. Both in life and after. Often, joy is the only thing that gives life any meaning. I don't want to give it up."

"Is there a paradise like that too?"

"There is any kind you like. Whatever you believe in, it exists. The real trick is to get there." She flicked her glowing ponytail behind her shoulder. "I don't even mind Purgatory that much. One can find anything they want or need here. What is really growing old for me is going back to Earth. I'm not sure what hell looks like, but let me tell you, some of the things I've seen in that good old world of ours couldn't be any worse than hell." She sighed.

I believed her. But I also missed the life I'd left behind. I took a big gulp of coffee, trying to keep the melancholy at bay.

"Well," I said. "After fourteen lifetimes, I can see how things can grow old."

"How many have you lived?" she asked.

"I have no idea."

"Oh," E smiled sheepishly. "I keep forgetting you're still alive."

We ate some more of the delicious food. The tray didn't contain any typical breakfast foods that I was used to, but the samples of finger foods from around our world provided for an excellent mix of tastes and textures, which I truly enjoyed.

"Please thank Gul for all this." I gestured at the now almost empty tray. "This is probably the best breakfast I've had, and I know a thing or two about cooking myself. I'm a chef."

"You are?" E glanced at me with interest.

"Well, I was. Back home."

E licked chocolate off her finger. "Gul will love to hear you enjoyed his cooking. Now..." She got up. "Let's get you into that dress, shall we? Unless you prefer to wear no clothes?"

No clothes was a valid option around here. But unlike E's nudity, mine would feel far more naked to me, with all its human details on display.

"I don't think I'll be comfortable running around without clothes," I confessed.

"Fair enough." She took the dress from the bed.

Printed with bright orange and gold designs, the dress had a long, voluminous skirt and a tight-fitting bodice. It was nothing I'd usually wear, even to a fancy event. But it was my only change of clothes at the moment. I promptly got out of my old outfit and let E put the dress on me, then lace it.

She took a step back, running an assessing gaze down my frame.

"It looks pretty on you."

"Thanks. I just wish I could get in and out of it on my own."

"I'll see if I can find something simpler next time. Sup is so over-the-top with all the outfits in his possession. This is prob- ably the least flashy thing he owns."

I smoothed my hands down the luxurious fabric of the skirt. Hopefully, I wouldn't spend long enough in Purgatory to worry about clothes. E had been chatty and forthcoming with answers to my questions. Maybe she could point me in the right direc- tion to escape.

"How long have you been in Purgatory?" I asked.

She tapped her chin with her finger.

"On and off, probably a century or two combined. This last time, it's been a few years already."

"So, you know this place well?"

"Like the back of my hand." She grinned confidently. "Things don't change much around here."

"Would you mind showing me around, then? If you aren't too busy."

"I'm never busy with something I can't set aside, but I doubt Avar would let you leave even for a little while."

"We don't need to tell him," I suggested. "Do we?"

She shook her head adamantly.

"Oh, we absolutely have to. If you sneak out, he'd raise a literal hell in Purgatory, trying to find you. This guy just doesn't know how to let go. The reason he doesn't ever have any souls living with him is because he couldn't suffer them leaving at the end."

"Has he been alone all his life?"

"Pretty much. I'm sure a random soul may drop by every now and then to keep him company for a night or two. But I haven't heard about anyone sticking around for longer than that."

5

Madison

Avar worked in the cluttered cave where he'd first made the bathroom for me last night. The bathroom had already been moved to my bedroom, but the clutter of relics and artifacts remained in the cave, filling it wall to wall and floor to ceiling.

As E and I entered, he slid an appreciative glance down my new dress.

"One thing Sup is really good at is beautifying even those who are already perfect," he muttered into his beard of tentacles before meeting my eyes. "Did you finish your breakfast? Can this meddlesome soul finally leave?"

E propped her hands on her ample hips. "I'm leaving, but I'm taking Madison for a walk around town—"

"Absolutely not," he cut her off.

"But what is she supposed to do here all day?" E pouted on my behalf. "Sit under the glass like one of your dried gnarly things and collect dust with all this clutter?"

He glanced around, following her gesture at the piles of stuff. "Well, she can help me clean this place."

"You need help?" I asked.

He nodded. "It'd be nice to have it all organized, displayed, and added to my collection eventually."

"Maybe if you didn't drag in everything you see, you wouldn't have the problem with having to organize so much stuff," I pointed out.

Avar's expression darkened; his tentacles twitched. The red glow of anger pulsed deep inside the purple. He clearly wasn't used to being criticized so frankly. I had the right to feel bitter. But unlike E, I wasn't just an immortal soul. I had a body to lose.

I braced for the worst, expecting him to lash out. Maybe I'd pushed too hard, but I had to know how far I could go with him, especially since I might have to spend a long time with this creature in the future.

He took a deep breath, visibly collecting himself, and the red glow dissolved into purple. Fortunately for me, the Sin of Greed seemed to have mastered self-control.

"I don't *drag in* just anything," he retorted somberly. "I collect exclusively rare and special pieces."

"Let's make a deal," I offered. "You'll let me go for a walk with E—" His hands surged in protest, his beard tentacles flared, but I lifted a finger, demanding he let me finish. "You'll allow me to learn more about Purgatory, since it's to become my home now against my will. And in return, I'll help you clean up around here, since it looks like no other soul wants to do it with you."

His brow jerked at the last barb in my words.

"Maybe it's *me* who doesn't want them around?" he barked.

"Either way..." I shrugged. "I'm already around. And it

appears I don't have anything else to do for the next few decades."

He hesitated.

"I can take you on a walk myself."

That wasn't what I wanted, though. I believed E would be more forthcoming with information that I needed to escape Purgatory. If Avar caught a whiff of my plans, he'd probably seal me into that glass box after all, both body and soul.

"I don't need a bodyguard or a babysitter, Avar," I said softly but firmly. "I just want to have a nice relaxing walk. If I can't do that, then what's the difference between your home and a prison for me?"

He fisted his hands, lashing with his tentacles so hard, they knocked off a crate with scrolls and threw a rolled rug across the cave.

I stood my ground, and E took pity on him.

"I'll keep an eye on her," she promised, soothingly. "And I'll have her back by lunchtime, with not a scratch on her precious body."

Settling his heavy stare on her, he said in a low, threatening voice, "If anything happens to Madison while she's with you, I'll personally see to it that you finally leave Purgatory for good. And this time, you won't return to Earth, nor will you go up to a paradise. You'll go *down*, E." He stabbed a finger downwards energetically, as if trying to poke a hole all the way to hell. "And you will stay down there for eternity."

The poor golden spirit gulped, her eyes opening wider. I decided not to run away while in E's company. Whether or not Avar indeed could deliver on his threats, I wasn't going to risk it and be the cause of her damnation.

"I'll be back," I promised, grabbing E's hand. "No need to threaten the only soul who's visited your place in who-knows-how long."

"Is he always like that?" I asked E as we walked down a path in the foothills dotted with bushes of blooming lilacs.

"You mean the insufferable grump?" E clarified. "Probably. But I don't know Avar that well. I've only been to his place a few times with his brothers and other souls when he allowed us to look at his collection. But he couldn't be all bad. Sins aren't strangers to virtues, after all, they're all siblings born to the same mother. Good is in Avar's essence somewhere. It just may be buried a little too deep for us to see."

We rounded the mountain, taking the path that ran between birch trees and flower-sprinkled clearings.

"No wonder he has no one," I concluded bitterly.

"Well, he has *you* for the next little while."

E's definition of "little while" differed from mine. She referred to the next few decades while I had every intention of escaping Avar's mountain at the first opportunity.

"Then of course, there are his brothers, his sisters, and Pandora," she said.

"Who?"

"Pandora, the mother of sins and virtues."

"Pandora is their mother? I didn't know that."

E tossed back her ponytail with a shrug. "Who else would unleash all the good and evil into the world just for fun? To see how it all plays out?"

"She doesn't sound like a good person," I muttered, climbing over a fallen tree trunk in our path.

"To be fair, Pandora is neither evil nor good, just bored. She stirs trouble to entertain herself. You know she's the one who brought a TV to Purgatory?"

I tripped over a knoll of grass. "The magical viewing box that Avar said his mother gifted them is just a TV?"

"It may be magical, but it works very much like a regular TV set, if you ask me." Unlike me, E navigated down the narrow path with ease. "It shows movies and TV shows, as well as many live streams from street cameras around the world. Sins rarely leave Purgatory. Avar sometimes does. So do Gul and Sup to get some things from our world. But all the others mostly stay here. So they're quite enjoying watching TV now."

"If the mortal sins stay here, how has there never been a shortage of wrath, or laziness, or envy in our world?"

"Do you think the sin brothers are responsible for people being mad or lazy?"

"Who else? How can there be so much anger on Earth, for example, if the Sin of Wrath spends all his time here, smelling lilacs in Purgatory?"

"There are no lilacs in Ira's lair," she corrected. "And Ira doesn't need to be in our world for people to feel angry. Humans are very capable of generating all the wrath they feel on their own. They just prefer to blame it on someone else."

E moved in light, bouncy steps, almost gliding over the rocky ground, easily scaling any obstacles. I suspected she could've walked twice as fast, but she slowed down for me to keep up.

"Anyway, most of the sins stayed in Purgatory until Pandora got them that viewing box. After they learned more about the modern world by watching it on the TV, some of them got curious about humans. Invi, for example, talked Avar into taking him along the last time. That's when they met you."

"Lucky me," I sighed.

She looked at me carefully. "It's not so bad here. Purgatory is a cute little town. Souls keep coming and going all the time, of course. But some stay for years or even decades. There are a few who have been stuck here for at least a century now."

"How big is this place?"

"Size is relative, isn't it?" she dismissed with a wave of a hand. "It's not like Purgatory has ever been measured."

"Why not?"

"No need. What does it matter? Either way, it has enough space to house every soul it takes."

As the trees receded with the forest staying behind us, the path widened into a rock paved road. It ran in the middle of a valley between hills studded with colorful buildings of every architectural style imaginable. Their appearance ranged from miniature palaces and high towers to log cabins or clay huts.

Souls moved between them. Some glowed with gold, like E, but most were different colors. Some even shimmered with iridescence, emitting every color of the spectrum.

The souls varied in size too. I gasped, pressing a hand to my chest as I spotted a tiny shape, not bigger than a toddler, slowly swinging on a swing in front of a house painted in purple and white.

"It's just a baby..." My voice hitched as my heart tightened painfully.

"Not necessarily." E petted my hand soothingly. "Looks don't matter here, remember? A soul is ageless and can take any form it wants. Some find comfort in the form of a child and may choose it after possibly a traumatic experience back in our world or if they need to contemplate the choices they've made in their past lives. Their smaller form is the sign for the rest of us to be gentle with them while they recover and return to their former selves."

As we passed by a quaint little cottage with a wide wrap-around porch set with wicker tables and chairs, someone waved at us from a table in the corner.

"Hi there, come have tea with me?" The lavender figure was one of the few in Purgatory who looked elderly, having taken the appearance of an older woman with light purple hair brushed up in a bun. She was also one of a handful who had clothes on, wearing a white, long-sleeved dress that was tied with a rope around her waist, bringing a monk's tunic to mind.

"Should we join her?" I asked E, unsure what the rules here were.

E nodded.

"It'd be rude not to." She led me to the patio. "This is Madison," she introduced me to the woman. "She just got here."

"I've heard." The woman gestured at the two empty chairs at her table. "Welcome to Purgatory, Madison. I'm Charity, a sister of the abomination who abducted you so heartlessly. I strongly disapprove of Avar's behavior, of course. Please tell me how I can make this experience more bearable for you."

I took a seat in the comfy wicker chair across the small round table from Charity. Her kind smile and warm lavender eyes put me at ease.

"I'm very glad to meet you," I said sincerely. "It has been a little...overwhelming, coming here."

The other souls at the tables on the porch stared at me. My solid body, with not a hint of any glow, stood out in this crowd like a twig in a bouquet of flowers. But no one bothered me with questions. Charity and E ignored the onlookers, so I did too. After a short while, they all went on about their business, chatting, drinking tea, and fluttering about while letting me be.

"It's understandable." Charity stirred sugar into her tea with a slim silver spoon. "You didn't plan to come here."

"No, not at all. I don't belong here."

She nodded. "You haven't finished what you were meant to do in your most current life. Some things are still tethering you to your old world, be it places, actions, or people. Souls with unfinished business don't rest. Unless…" She paused, filling the silence with a hidden meaning.

"Unless I leave?" I finished for her, anxiously.

"Or find a new purpose."

"What kind of purpose?"

Charity put down the spoon and turned to E, who sat next to me. "Dearest, would you be so sweet as to get Madison some tea, please? You and I don't need to eat, but our new friend may be hungry."

After the scrumptious breakfast that morning, I wasn't hungry at all, but I didn't protest, wondering what Charity was up to.

Too restless to stay in one place for too long, E got to her feet eagerly. "I'll be right back."

"Take your time, sweetie," Charity called after her. "There is no need to hurry."

The moment E went inside the cottage, Charity leaned toward me across the table.

"What happened to you was outrageous, Madison." She lowered her voice for only me to hear. "But you can use this opportunity to do the right thing."

"What do you mean?"

"Avar is my brother. And I should love him, despite all his shortcomings. But he's done a lot of wrong in his life. He's been taking things that don't belong to him."

"Don't I know that?" I exhaled a humorless laugh.

"But you can help me return what he's stolen."

"How? I'm just a human. A mortal one, at the moment. I have no power. And frankly, I'm still feeling a little dazed and confused in this world of yours."

"But you're also the only, um…well, the only *animated exhibit* in Avar's collection. You see…" She stirred eagerly. "He rigorously guards his collection. He hardly ever leaves it. Until now, no one has been allowed to stay on his mountain. But since he has you, we have a perfect opportunity."

"For what?"

"To return everything to their rightful owners."

"Without Avar's knowledge or permission?" I winced. "Do you want me to help you rob your brother?"

She huffed impatiently. "It's for the greater good, my dear. I've seen your past life—"

"You have? How?"

"Everything you do is recorded for the future decisions of the Higher Judgment. You are a good, generous person. You help others without expecting rewards. You love to give. You know that returning to people what's rightfully theirs is the proper thing to do. It's not a robbery when one takes what has been stolen."

"I-I'm not sure, if you put it that way…" My head was spinning, with Charity's words turning in it in a twister.

"Madison." She leaned closer, covering my hand with hers. "Do you have any idea what invaluable treasures Avar's collection holds? I'm not talking about gold and diamonds, though I'm sure he has plenty of those too. He has the results of medical studies that, if published, would potentially improve the lives of many people, including children. He has poems and novels that your world has never seen. There are historical accounts and original writings of souls who will never again return to your world, having long departed either to hell or paradise—because both house plenty of geniuses." She squeezed my hand emphatically. "All these treasures were created by humans for the benefit of humanity. My brother has no right to keep them all to himself."

"But—"

"Please understand," she continued, not letting me put a word of doubt in, "Mortal humans are such wretched creatures.

They have so little, just trying to make it through their current lifetimes. Don't you think it's beyond cruel to take their things from them?" She blinked rapidly, as if struggling to control the impending tears.

E strolled from the open front door of the cottage, carrying a porcelain teapot in one hand and a small silver tray with dishes in the other.

Charity promptly leaned back in her chair.

"You don't have to give me an answer right now, Madison." She gave me a gentle smile. "But please, think about it."

E placed the tray in the middle of the table. "Sorry for the delay. I ran into a few familiar souls and had to catch up."

"No need to apologize, sweetie." Charity took a sip of her tea. "We have plenty of time."

"Not really." E sat in her chair while I thanked her. "We can't drink tea here forever. If I don't bring Madison back by lunchtime, Avar will rip my head off, figuratively and likely literally too." She rubbed her neck with a grimace. "If there is anything else you want to see in town, Madison, we'd better go soon."

"Just a minute." I wondered if I could be open with Charity. She'd said she felt bad for her brother's abducting me and even offered to make my situation more bearable. Maybe she could help? "If someone doesn't belong to Purgatory, can they leave here?"

Charity lifted her cup to her lips.

"Of course they can," she replied. "Purgatory isn't a prison." E cleared her throat at that, and Charity added, "It's merely a holding point for the souls who need time for reflection."

"How could one leave here then?" I prompted, halting my breath in anticipation of her answer.

"Oh, that's easy," she said to my utter shock. "There're

many ways into Purgatory but the only way out is through the Gates." She pointed with her teaspoon down the rock-paved road.

Hope made a summersault in my chest.

"The Gates? How do I find them?"

"Finding them is simple, just follow the main road until you leave the town. However, passing through them can be difficult. Souls can leave only according to the decisions of the Higher Judgment."

E frowned. "The Gates are quite a way from here. We won't make it back in time.

Trust me, there isn't much to see that way, anyway. I've been turned away from the Gates enough times to assure you they are a boring sight."

"But..." I protested. "I shouldn't be here in the first place. I don't belong to Purgatory."

"Do you want to leave?" E shifted uneasily, glancing at the purple mountain in the distance.

"Not right now," I assured her. "I don't want Avar to rip your head off. But I will find a way to get away from him sooner or later. Even if it's the last thing I do."

"You have the right to leave whenever you want," Charity waved E's concerns off. "All you have to do is to pass through the Gates."

"And that's it?" I couldn't believe the escape was that easy.

"For a soul, that's all there is." Charity smiled. "You'll go back to your world, and Avar will get the mortal body he so desperately wants."

Her last statement made me pause.

"What do you mean? How is he going to get my body?"

"Only a soul can get through the Gates, sweetie," Charity patiently explained.

Dread pressed heavily on my chest with the realization. "I'd have to give up my body..."

She nodded. "Since you haven't died yet, your soul is free to go back. But a body can't travel through the Gates. You'll have to leave it behind."

I slid my hands down my thighs, the gesture I'd made many times when wiping my hands on my apron after cleaning or doing dishes.

I liked my body. It had enabled me to put in long shifts at the restaurant, helping me lift my business off the ground. It had given me pleasure with some of my past boyfriends, and even more so with my vibrator. I liked dressing it up when going out with friends on rare but always fun occasions and treating it to a long relaxing bath afterwards.

My body felt comfy and familiar, like a pair of well-worn jeans. I was not ready to part with it.

"You'll get a new body," E said optimistically, clearly trying to cheer me up. "It'll be a cute one, too, because all bodies start out as babies, and babies are adorable."

I stared straight ahead, feeling more lost than ever. My heart got heavier with every breath I took. "I'll have to live a completely new life then? With strangers?"

"But they won't be strangers once you get there," Charity said breezily. "You'll be their baby."

"Hopefully, they'll love you and take care of you," E added. "You'll get a brand-new life that could be worse than what you had, but could also be better."

"A new life..." I echoed.

I felt like a sail without the wind, a boat set adrift with no direction, and I couldn't take a single step anywhere.

"Oh, Madison..." E wrapped her arm around my shoulders. "It's just a body. Changing it isn't much harder than changing clothes. Trust me, I've had fourteen of them. A body is important while you have it, but once you leave it, it doesn't matter at all. Sometimes, it's actually a relief to get rid of it." She moved her shoulders as if shrugging out of a heavy coat.

"It's not about the body, E. It's about everything and everyone I left behind. Like my mom…" My voice broke, and I had to inhale deeply before continuing. "I can't believe I'll never see her again."

"Oh, but you can," Charity promised. "If she loves you as much as you love her and wants to see you again, sooner or later you'll run into each other either here or out there, beyond the Gates. You may not even wait for her that long. How old was your mother when you left? Was she in poor health?"

I believed Charity meant well, but her implying that my mom needed to die for me to see her again made me sob in misery. I buried my face in my hands.

"Oh God, Madison, please don't cry," E begged. "We really should be going back to the mountain now. It's probably lunchtime already. Maybe if you ate something you'd feel better? Food always used to put me in a better mood when I had a body."

"I'm not hungry." I sniffled, wiping away the tears that rolled down my cheeks, only for new ones to run right after them.

"Oh no…" E squeaked. "We're too late."

I followed her gaze down the road to the mountain. Avar's tall purple figure was moving our way.

"Well, um…" E jumped to her feet. "I probably should go?"

I nodded. There was no need to keep her here, risking Avar's wrath. If he was angry, he could take it out on me.

"Bye, Avar." She wiggled her fingers in his direction, then ran off, giving him a wide berth.

He paid her no attention, heading straight to me. As he

scooped me from my chair with his tentacles. I pushed with my hands against his chest, forcing him to hold me away from him.

"You're crying," he boomed, taking in my tear-stained cheeks, then glared at Charity. "Why is she upset?"

Charity finished her tea deliberately slowly before setting down her cup.

"Do you really have no idea why a soul you stole from the only life she knew would be crying in distress?"

He shifted on his feet uneasily, rubbing the back of his neck.

"She was fine this morning," he said.

Charity tilted her head mockingly. "Was she? Or are you just too obtuse to recognize a suffering soul?"

"Madison?" He ducked his head, seeking my eyes. "Tell me, what's happening?"

I turned away, refusing to meet his eyes.

"What's happening?" Charity echoed with sarcasm. "Nothing, really, other than a boorish sin ruining her life. Greed destroys the world, brother. And you're the root of it all."

Avar shot her a glare from under his thick eyebrows.

"I see you're just as severe and rigid in your *virtue* as ever, sister," he snapped. His voice thundered. "I've never asked you for anything, Charity. I don't need your love, not even your understanding. But you will stay away from Madison from now on, do you hear me? If I ever see her crying in your company again, I'll make you pay for every tear she sheds."

Charity stood up, tall and proud, with her white robe billowing in the breeze blowing over the porch of the teahouse.

"You have no one to blame for her tears, but yourself," she retorted.

He heaved a sigh, turning away.

"I know," he muttered under his breath. "Believe me, I do."

"You think you're all-powerful, Avar, but there is judgement coming for you too!" Charity yelled after him as he stomped away toward his mountain, carrying me in the tight embrace of his tentacles.

My tired arms gave in. I stopped trying to push him away, and Avar pressed me to his chest at last.

With a finger under my chin, he turned my face to him.

"Tell me what upset you? And why?"

"*You're* asking me *why?*" I met his deep purple eyes. "How dare you? Charity is certainly not the one to blame here. All she did was just tell me the truth. I'm trapped here. For the rest of my life. There is no hope for an escape..." My voice broke off, and I went silent, refusing to cry in front of him again.

He had the decency to look ashamed, letting go of my chin. I used the moment to appeal to that newly discovered decency of his.

"Take me back, Avar, please. Get a stray cat instead or adopt a dog if you're lonely. A pet has a body, too, and will be a true friend for you. Please, let me go."

"I don't know how," he admitted, looking at me sincerely. "I don't know how to let go of what I have. I can't part from you. If I try, I fear I'll cease to exist."

He was Greed—an entity whose very essence was to acquire and possess. He took and never let go. Escaping him would be like trying to climb out of a black hole, working against its cosmic effort of sucking everything in.

Understanding of it came crashing down on me. There was no use in crying when faced with a black hole. Nothing would compel the Sin of Greed to do what he was simply incapable of doing.

A tentacle slithered around my shoulders in a gesture probably meant to comfort, but I shrugged it away.

"Put me down."

To my surprise, he listened, carefully setting me on the mountain path, then

walked slowly next to me, matching my pace as I dragged my feet through the foothills.

"I can't take you back, Madison," he started.

"Yeah, yeah, I get it," I waved him off, feeling exhausted, both physically and emotionally.

"But I can give you a good life here, Madison, a much better life than many souls have back in your world. With me, you'll want for nothing. If there is anything you need or want, anything at all, let me know and I'll find a way to get it for you."

He spoke earnestly. My unhappiness obviously bothered him. For what it was worth, Avar didn't want me to suffer. I believed that deep inside, he wished to fix what he had done to me. Sadly, he lacked the ability to do it.

The only reason he could deliver on his promise to give me anything I wished for was because I already belonged to him. His giving me things meant he'd be adding to his collection, not losing anything. That was the only way he could give, the closest he could come to being generous.

"Thanks," I mumbled, tripping over a tree root that crossed the path.

Avar's tentacle whipped around my middle to steady me. I lifted my hands up, not touching it, and he promptly removed it from me.

"It's a long way up the mountain, and you look tired," he noted. "Let me carry you."

I glanced up the path that wound between hills and trees. It was a long way up indeed.

He noticed my hesitation and added, "Just my arms. I'll keep my tentacles away, I promise."

I didn't mean to make my apprehension of those appendages of his so obvious. The two thick undulating tentacles, covered with round, translucent suckers like silver coins, extended from his sides, just under his arms. Avar used them along with his arms, and they certainly seemed handy. I felt uneasy about their snake-like appearance. But the tentacles were a part of him, and I hated for him to think that his looks repulsed me in any way.

"It's fine," I said. "I don't mind the tentacles."

I let him lift me with one arm and settle me against his chest. As he headed up the mountain, his steady pace lulled me, helping me relax. I rested my head on his wide shoulder. He promptly shifted away the slim appendages of his beard too. These didn't have suckers and were about as thick as my wrist at their base, tapering down at the ends, smooth and flexible.

"Did you have children back in your past life, Madison?" he asked unexpectedly.

I raised my head from his shoulder and blinked.

"No."

"A soulmate, maybe?"

"You mean like a boyfriend or a husband?"

"Possibly, but not necessarily."

"No. I was still looking for one of those when you snatched me."

"Tell me, then, what is holding you back? Why do you wish to return so badly when most souls view going back to that world as a nuisance or even a punishment?"

"I have people in my life, Avar. They depend on me."

"How? In what way?"

"I have a restaurant that I started from scratch, using the inheritance I got from my grandma. It included her collection of recipes too. Grandma was the one who taught me how to cook. I went to culinary college because of her. I knew all her recipes by heart, and I always knew I wanted to share her food with others. So, I did." It wasn't a simple, straightforward answer to his question, but he listened patiently, so I kept talking. "Running a restaurant hasn't been easy. I still spend more than I make. But we've built a small community around my business. My employees are like family to me. Every one of them was struggling before I gave them the job, and I'm so happy to be in the position to help."

"How could you help if you just said you were struggling yourself? You made less than you spent. How long could that even last?"

I noticed he spoke in past tense, so I switched too. It made sense since that life remained only in my past now.

"No one at the restaurant knew how hard it was for me to keep that place afloat. I paid my guys well. They had job security and full benefits. For me, it was just money. For them, it was a good life, not just survival. And it paid off too. I had zero turnover in the past two years. The restaurant was doing much better lately. I believed I would've climbed out of debt sometime down the road. I worked hard for it. I hadn't taken a single day off since the opening day and worked twelve-hour shifts all the time."

I sighed with a pang of regret. I wished I could see the restaurant thrive one day. Now, there was no hope for me to ever see it happen. According to the instructions in my letter that Avar had delivered to my mom last night, she'd be getting ready to sell the place now.

"So, you paid your people generously, even when you made no money?" he asked.

"I did more than that," I said proudly. "I paid for many other things that people do for their friends and family, like holiday parties, Christmas bonuses, wedding presents. Like I said, it's just money." I shrugged. "People's happiness is far more important."

"Not if you struggle yourself to make them happy," he

disagreed. "I don't know how your employees felt, of course. But if you had to put yourself through hardship to make *my* life easier, I would want to know what it costs you. And frankly, I wouldn't accept your help until I know for sure you don't need help yourself."

I bit my lip. "Well, that's just you. You're not human."

"True, but I still believe that your friends should know what you're giving up in order to gift them all those parties and presents. After all, if you fail, they will all fail with you. You can do so much more for others if you ensure your own survival first."

I rested my head on his shoulder again, pondering his words. Shielding my friends and family from my financial troubles had always felt like the right thing to do. Would Claire or Sam want to know what it cost me to help them with money for their relatives? But what would they do if they knew?

What if they already knew, anyway? After all, everyone saw that I was at the restaurant day and night. Everyone knew I hadn't taken a vacation since we opened. Did they care? Ultimately, it wasn't their responsibility to make sure I didn't collapse from exhaustion or get crushed under a mountain of debt. It was no one's job but mine.

"In your world, you had to take care of yourself," Avar echoed my thoughts. "Especially if you wanted to be fit to take care of others. Here, however, you don't need to worry about anything." He gently cradled my head against his shoulder. "Here, I will take care of you."

6

Madison

Making good on my promise the very next day, I started helping Avar with cleaning out the cluttered cave and adding the stored items to his collection.

The contents of every crate, trunk, and box had to be unloaded and cataloged into a long, wide scroll that Avar kept locked up somewhere. Then, each item had to be numbered, signed, and displayed in a cabinet or a shelf of Avar's choosing. It was a long and meticulous process, but also extremely interesting because every item Avar had held a story.

After three days of working from breakfast to lunch and from lunch to dinner, we had barely made a dent in this pile of treasures, but I genuinely enjoyed the work. Finding new and unusual things proved exciting. Opening a trunk always held a fantastic surprise, making me feel like a kid on Christmas morning.

"Wow." I lifted a heavy, leather-bound tome out of a box. "This is by far the heaviest book I've ever held."

"Let me help you." Avar reached out a tentacle for assistance, then quickly replaced it with his hand instead.

He'd been using his tentacles sparingly and cautiously around me, mostly keeping them behind his back. I'd told him I hardly noticed them anymore, but it wasn't entirely true. I found his tentacles fascinating and furtively watched him using them as he unpacked trunks or organized items on a shelf.

I let him take the book from me, and he opened the cover. His eyes moved as he read the title, then his right tentacle gently covered the page, one of the small round suckers on its underside attached to the parchment, and Avar carefully turned the page with it.

His arm tentacles carried out routine functions, similar to his arms and hands. The slim tentacles of his beard, or as he called them his "feelers," worked more like fingers, allowing him to learn additional things about an object by a more detailed touch.

As I spent more time with him, I also learned that Avar's feelers often reflected his mood. They draped over his chest loosely when he was content and happy, trembled when he was on edge, and flared out in a semi-circle when he was angry or irritated.

Right now, the tips of the feelers gently glided over the open pages of the book in his hands, as if trying to learn more than what the words written on it could tell.

"What's it about?" I asked.

In Purgatory, I discovered I could read any language, but I'd only glimpsed the title of the book before giving it to Avar. It read *My Fantastic Travels Between the Worlds of the River of Mists.*

"It's written by a werewolf named Evior," Avar said, "who

came to Earth from the world called Nerifir, using the portal through the magical River of Mists. He writes about his adventures."

"A werewolf? So, it's fiction, then?"

"I'm sure the author enhanced some of his adventures to make his story more interesting, but I believe most of it is true."

I laughed incredulously. "How can adventures of a werewolf be true if werewolves don't exist?"

"They don't exist in your world, Madison. Or, more accurately, they aren't indigenous to your world. But they do come from other places, occasionally. I brought this book from your world a few centuries ago, just never got around to putting it away."

"Did you steal it?" I couldn't help asking.

I hadn't accepted Charity's proposition, and it had little to do with Avar or her but everything to do with me. Her cause might be noble. I owed no loyalty to Avar, either. But if he did something wrong, I felt he should be held accountable for it openly. His collection should be seized and dismantled in accordance with whatever laws this place had. Sneaking behind Avar's back to help Charity steal from him didn't appeal to me. Despite her reassurances, her offer appalled me. But I couldn't get my conversation with her out of my head.

Humanity's biggest treasures might be hiding in this very cave. Did Avar have any right to keep them away from the world?

"I didn't *steal* it," he protested. "I *took* it just before the author was going to burn it to avoid being discovered as a werewolf living in the human world. I replaced it with a blank copy to be burned and kept the original. It has never been read by a single soul other than the author himself."

"You haven't read it either, then? Has it just been sitting here all this time?"

With a sheepish expression, he ran a hand down the back of his head. "I have collected a considerable number of books. Even with me reading every day, there simply isn't enough time to get through them all in a timely fashion."

I knew what that was like. I had a long list of books I wished to read, too, eventually, when the restaurant was more settled, and I could finally take a day off or maybe have a proper vacation one day.

Now, it occurred to me, I had all the time I'd ever need.

"Do you mind if I keep the book for a little while then? I'd like to read it."

The idea of other worlds beside ours intrigued me. I wished to learn more, especially from someone who came from another world—a werewolf.

"You can have anything you want, Madison. Everything I own is for you to use."

"Thank you." I put the book next to a large pink shell that had a poem in a long-lost language carved into its spiral.

"Now, let's see what else we have in here." Avar leaned over the open trunk we'd been unpacking.

With him sitting on the floor, his shoulder was at my chest level. I hugged his arm from behind and placed my chin on his shoulder to see what else was in the trunk. He shifted his tentacle out of my way, then patted my arm with his hand before removing a bundle of scrolls tied with a leather cord.

We'd spent a lot of time together in the past three days, working side by side like this. Being close to him no longer intimidated me. Maybe it was the natural attraction of a sin that lured me closer to him, but I felt increasingly more comfortable around Avar.

The mountain shook unexpectedly, the tremor rolling through the air. My heart leaped in my chest in fright. I grabbed onto Avar for balance. His tentacle immediately whipped around me to keep me upright.

"Is it dinnertime already?" he asked. "This must be E with your food."

"You really should consider installing a doorbell or something," I muttered, leaning away from him to test my legs after the fright.

E had been delivering food twice a day now, in the morning and in the evening, also leaving me a sandwich and some snacks for the day. Yet I still hadn't gotten used to the dramatic reaction of the mountain to her visits.

Since I failed to escape Purgatory, I feared I'd be depending on Gul's meals for a very long time now. Thankfully, Avar assured me that Gul loved cooking, and E seemed to like popping in for a chat. But when I'd mentioned that I would be happy to cook my own meals without inconveniencing anyone, Avar also promised to build me a kitchen on his mountain.

"Are you alright?" Avar made sure I was stable on my own two feet. "Sorry, I can see how the shaking can be annoying. But I never had so many visits before, hardly any. Just wait here. I'll let her in."

He turned to me from the exit, and I took in his tall figure. He had no bones or muscles inside, yet he was shaped as if he did. Human imagination created him as a monster, but it used the shape of a man as the starting point.

Avar had wide shoulders, thick upper arms with the definition of the biceps, and a well-built torso with the grid that mimicked abdominal muscles in the stomach area. He even had the perfectly shaped V-muscle in his lower belly that guided my attention downwards. It was only a tease, however. The space between his legs remained modestly smooth.

I blinked, catching myself very *im*modestly ogling a mortal sin.

"I'll stay right here," I promised. "Not going anywhere."

"Be careful with some of these things," he warned on his way out.

With Avar gone, the cave felt too big and empty, despite all the clutter. Searching for a distraction, I glanced back into the trunk. After Avar had removed the scrolls, a beautiful box came into view. Made from golden filigree and set with polished gems and mother-of-pearl, it looked like a jewelry box.

Kneeling by the trunk, I got the box out. It was roughly the size of a book and not locked. Inside the box, a pretty jewelry set nestled in soft black velvet—a large ring with a flower of pink gemstones for petals and a matching choker necklace.

The ring was big enough to fit my thumb. I moved my hand, admiring how the light of the lanterns in the cave played in the pink crystal flower. The design of the piece was simple. Its beauty lay in the stones. They sparkled and shined, breaking the bright light of the lanterns into fireworks of sparks.

I took the choker out too. It looked like a collar, with the pink stone flowers arranged in a golden setting and a heart-shaped clasp on the back. A thin golden chain extended from the bottom point of the heart. It was long enough to probably reach past my waist if I had the necklace on.

As big as the ring was, the collar seemed small, and I wondered if it would fit me. I wrapped it around my neck. Surprisingly, the clasp closed just fine. The collar fit snugly but not uncomfortably so. The golden chain stretched down my back under my dress, tickling against my spine.

The stones of the ring cast a shimmer on my thumb that made my skin appear to glow like a soul...or a sin. I looked around for a mirror, wondering if the choker left the same glowing effect on my neck.

As I turned around, the chain stroked along my back, sending a shiver of pleasure down my body. My neck warmed under the collar, the heat trickling downwards in a rush of tingles. I inhaled slowly, fighting a sudden wave of dizziness.

Where did that come from? Was I coming down with a bug or something?

Yet I didn't feel sick or tired. I felt energized and invigorated. Every nerve in my body seemed to be coming awake, making every sensation so much more acute.

I was hyperaware of each breath I took and every movement I made. The fine fabric of my dress rubbed against my skin. The stimulation caused a sizzling wave of desire to rush through me. My nipples hardened, poking against the silky fabric.

Voices approached from the path leading up the mountain. E chatted away with Avar, who replied in grunts or monosyllables.

They'd be here soon.

Alarm sent another wave of heat through me from my neck down my body. I tore the ring off my thumb and tossed it back into the box. Frantically, I searched for the closure of the collar, but I couldn't find the stone heart with my trembling fingers.

With the dress brushing against my nipples, heat pooled between my legs. I pressed my thighs together, trying to alleviate the pressure building up in my core. It didn't help. My inner muscles clenched with need, instantly drenching my underwear.

"I can't stay long," E's voice reached me from outside of the cave.

"Good," Avar boomed in response.

"Gul is having a dinner party at his place. Everyone is coming. You and Madison were also invited, by the way."

"I know. But we aren't going anywhere. We have work to do."

"Maybe you should at least let Madison come with me? I'll —" Her voice cut off abruptly as they both rounded the corner and saw me on my knees on the floor.

The chaffing of the dress against my extremely sensitive skin became unbearable. I'd opened as many buttons on the back as I could reach and tugged the fabric off my shoulders.

"I...I can't," I tried to explain to Avar and E as they both stared at me from the entrance of the cave. "I need this off. I need..." I yanked at the dress, making it slide down to my waist, then freed my arms from it.

The cool air brushed over my bare breasts, but instead of a relief, it sent another charge of lust through my body. I moaned, shamelessly loud. Avar's hands flexed into fists, and I imagined him squeezing my breasts or gripping my hips like that with desperation.

The liquid heat inside me spilled over, trickling down my thighs. I shoved my skirt between my legs with one hand while squeezing my breast with another. The nipple got trapped between my fingers. The pinch sent me into a lust frenzy, with my thighs trembling.

"What's happening to me?" I whimpered.

Avar promptly ran his eyes over me, stopping at the collar around my neck. His frown deepened.

"You'll need help."

"Oh, I think I'll stay longer, after all," E cooed, inching closer.

Avar lashed a tentacle across her way, stopping her in her tracks.

"Leave."

"But you said she needs help," E protested. "I'm happy to help."

"I'll take care of it. You have to go. Now." He turned her around and ushered her down the path back to the mountain's entrance.

I didn't care much whether she went or stayed. Lust clouded my mind and judgment. Need throbbed through my entire body, making me shake.

Deep inside, however, under the hot lava of scorching desire, I felt grateful to Avar for making sure there were as few witnesses as possible to whatever was happening to me.

I couldn't even think anymore. All I wanted was for this to be over, and at the same time, I didn't want it to end. Heat coursed and tingled through me. Pleasure rippled in waves with a promise of more.

If only I could get rid of this dress. I gathered the skirt around me and lifted it over my head. The waist part stuck around my breasts. I tugged. Then, I felt someone else tug with me, pulling the dress finally off.

"Avar." I came face to face with my mortal sin. Sitting back on his haunches, with my dress in his lap, he looked like a savior to me. "I'm afraid I need to be fucked," I begged, my eyes open wide with horror at my own words. "Now. Please."

What was I asking him to do? Sex was not supposed to happen between us. I had made it clear the very first day we met.

Right now, however, my biggest concern was that he wouldn't do it. Or that he couldn't.

"I need..." I whimpered.

"I know." He put my dress aside.

"It's the collar, isn't it?"

"Yes." He heaved a sigh. "You shouldn't have touched it."

"Can you take it off? I can't..." I slid my fingers around the necklace to the back of my neck, but the clasp seemed to disappear completely. The stones merged together into one solid piece of rock, circling my neck in a chokehold.

Avar took my hands from the collar and placed them in my lap. The heat from his touch rocked me with another jolt of lust, burning shame to ashes.

"Oh God, I have to..." I slid my hand between my legs and found the spot that throbbed so violently. When I pressed against it, however, the need surged higher with no relief in sight.

Avar took my hand in his, stopping me from touching myself.

"You can't do anything about it on your own, sweetheart," he said softly. "If you try, you may hurt yourself. If you don't, lust will burn your body until it perishes."

I squirmed, rubbing my thighs together but to no avail.

"Help me. Please."

"I will," he assured me somberly. "But I don't want you to hate me for it after the spell is gone, or to hate yourself. I won't fuck you, and I'll only touch you where it's completely necessary to bring you relief."

I nodded quickly, eager to feel his hands on me again.

He cupped my chin, bringing my face to his until our eyes met.

"It's not your fault, Maddy. It needs to be done," he said slowly, pausing after each sentence to make sure I heard and understood him. "I have no choice. There is only one way to help you. I will have to make you come. For as many times as necessary until the spell is over."

It was hard to focus on his words. My awareness almost entirely narrowed down to the sensation of his hand under my chin. Desire clouded my mind, thicker than intoxication. Eventually, the meaning of what he was saying filtered through to me, and I nodded.

"Okay." I leaned forward.

His tentacles circled me without touching. Standing on my knees, I grabbed one, partially to steady myself, partially because I craved his touch more than my next breath.

"Oh God, Avar... I feel like I'm dying."

"I won't let you die, dearest." Sitting on the floor, he carefully placed me on his lap.

His one hand supported my back. With the other, he parted my knees, and I opened my legs for him eagerly.

Carefully, he slid a hand up my thigh. The tip of his thick finger connected with my most sensitive spot, sending an explosion of pleasure through my entire body from my fingertips to my toes. I screamed, arching my back.

"Hush, Maddy," he said softly. "I'll make it better."

I pressed my legs together, trapping his hand between my thighs. But the throbbing heat in my core proved uncontainable. I snapped my legs back open again, craving release.

"More... Please."

He worked me with the tip of his finger. His initial frown of concentration relaxed. His movements became more fluid. He circled the swollen bud between my legs, the press of his finger bringing both pleasure and pain. Both grew to unbearable levels so fast, I really feared I might die from desire.

Sensation crested, and Avar set off my orgasm. I gripped his tentacle, thrusting my hips into his touch.

"Just like that, my sweet girl," he murmured.

Climax rocked through me like an explosion. If Avar wasn't holding me, I'd roll off his lap and crash to the floor. A warm wave of relief flooded me right after, allowing me to relax and draw a long breath at last.

"Feeling better?" Avar asked, placing his warm palm on my thigh.

"A little," I smiled, panting and shaking violently.

It had happened fast and brutally strong. My body still trembled from head to toe, but I felt a little calmer now.

Was it over?

Could I take the collar off?

At that very moment, however, I didn't wish to stir a muscle, relaxing in Avar's lap, warm and comfortable.

Lazily, I ran my fingers along his tentacle. The translucent suckers dotted its underside like tiny jellyfish. When I poked one in its center, the delicate circle closed around my finger, hugging it tightly.

I smiled. "Your suckers tickle."

"*Corollas*," he corrected. "In my case, they're called corollas. I thought my tentacles repulsed you," he added.

"They don't," I protested. "Not anymore. They looked unusual to me in the beginning. But now..." I touched another delicate corolla with the tip of my nose, and it wrapped around it gently. "Well, it's still unusual," I laughed. "But I don't mind it." I rubbed my cheek against the tentacle. "I don't mind any part of you, Avar."

"That is definitely the collar speaking," he dismissed. "Humans gave the sins a monstrous appearance specifically to repulse and intimidate, so you would stay away."

"Is that so?" I climbed to my feet, standing up in his lap. In this position, his head was slightly below mine. I'd never been this close to him before and now used the chance to explore his features. "Let me see. What exactly makes you a monster, Avar? Thick, bushy eyebrows. Fierce purple eyes. Tentacles for a beard."

"These are feelers," he said. "They don't have corollas, see?"

I didn't think that made a big difference but didn't argue, cupping his face.

"Whoever created you should've tried harder if they

wanted you to repulse me. From the very first day I met you, Avar, there has always been a pull that I had to fight. Your calm, quiet kindness to me is drawing me closer every day, and nothing about your looks can stop it. Not your bald head." I slid my palms up his temples. "Not even all these horns." I ran my fingers up the ridged curves of his front horns.

He sucked in a breath and tossed his head back with a tortured groan.

"Not the horns. Please, sweetheart, don't touch the horns," he begged.

I jerked my hands away as if from a hot stove.

"What happened? What did I do?"

He pressed his fingers against my wrists, gently moving my hands further away from his head.

"Not the horns, sweetheart," he repeated firmly.

"Did I hurt you?"

Without a body like mine, Avar didn't have a nervous system. He couldn't feel physical pain. But I knew him enough to understand he had emotions, and emotional pain often felt worse than any physical wound.

"No," he exhaled a strangled breath. "Let's just say I wish to keep control around you, and it'd be infinitely harder to do so if you were to caress my horns."

"Um..." Then it dawned on me. "Oooh. Is that how you get excited? When someone touches your horns?"

I licked my lips, eyeing his horns with a new appreciation. There had been something especially enthralling in that groan of his when I'd touched them. I wanted to see Avar going completely undone. I wished to get lost in that passion along with him.

Need vibrated inside me, growing stronger again. Even through its fog, however, I forced myself to respect his plea, staying away from his horns.

"It's happening again," I whimpered, pressing my shivering body into his warmth.

"It should be over by morning," he said soothingly. "We'll just have to manage it until then."

He found the golden chain dangling from the collar along my spine and wound the end of it around his finger. His tentacles slipped up my legs, then up my sides. My desire spiked higher. Avar knew how to distract me from his horns. All I could think about now was the renewed throbbing between my legs.

He cupped my backside with his hand and coiled a tentacle around my middle. Its tip stroked my breasts, the corollas gently plucking at my nipples. Heat trickled down my body from his touch and from the cursed collar.

I leaned into him, my hands combing through the feelers of his beard.

"Why won't you fuck me, Avar?" I craved to feel him everywhere on and inside me.

He circled my opening with his finger.

"Well, for one, this sweet, little hole of yours is way too small for my cock, darling."

"So, you do have a cock."

"I do. But it'd be way too big for a delicate thing like you." He leaned into my neck, his beard feelers skittering along my sensitive skin.

I moaned, gripping his shoulders.

"Kiss me, Avar," I begged, delirious with lust.

"No, sweetheart." He slipped a finger inside me. It was at least twice as thick as my thumb, prompting me to spread my legs wider.

"Why not?" I demanded, riding his finger. "You said you own my body already. You may as well have it now."

"If I claim you in every way, you're mine, body and soul,

then no one will be able to pry you away from me. Is that what you want?"

Judging by his tone, the question was rhetorical. He didn't expect an answer, but I actually considered it. At that moment, I wanted him so badly, I would sell my soul for a kiss.

Thankfully, he was thinking rationally for both of us.

"You can have my hand, Maddy." He pumped harder. "Nothing else."

Pressing a thumb to my clit, he set off another mind-blinding orgasm. I came just as hard as before. My legs shook, my knees buckled. I fell against his chest, supported only by his tentacle around my waist.

He withdrew his hand and licked the finger that had been inside me. I arched an eyebrow in silent question, and he smirked in response.

"Just because I can't have the whole meal doesn't mean I can't have a little taste. You are delicious, my dear," he murmured, lapping off my juices from his finger. "Inside and out."

Spent, I relaxed against his chest, trying to catch my breath.

"Rest now," he murmured, getting up and taking me with him. "It'll start again before you know it."

"Where are you taking me?"

"To bed."

"But my bed is that way." I lifted my hand but had no strength left to point in the right direction, dropping it back on his shoulder.

"I know. But your bed is too small for me. I'm taking you to my room."

7

Avar

"This is your bedroom?" Maddy gasped, twisting in my arms.

I'd claimed the west side of the mountain for my bedroom, so I could watch the sunset every night. Few souls had visited my mountain. Even fewer had been here, in the space that was entirely mine.

A shiver of unease ran down my spine as I crossed the threshold with Maddy in my arms. The sensation was similar to the mountain's trembling when invaded. Invasion of my personal space always was insufferable. But Maddy had to be made comfortable. She needed a bed. And since I had to stay with her, I needed space too.

My bed would accommodate us both comfortably. It stood in the middle of my room under the natural skylights on the side of the mountain with four granite columns for bed posts.

The flowers of the glowing vines that stretched between the columns absorbed the sunlight through the day, and now glowed with soft purple light, emitting a fragrant golden shimmer. The golden sparks reflected in Maddy's dark-brown eyes.

"You sleep here?" she marveled. "This place looks like it's from a fairy tale. But then again, the entire Purgatory looks like a fairy tale, doesn't it?"

I ran the tip of one of my tentacles down her arm, and she smiled. With the purple glow reflecting off her warm, honey-brown skin and the golden sparks dancing in her eyes, she looked like a fairy princess herself.

Travan's collar pulsed pink around her neck. Maddy's pupils dilated, and her eyes widened with a puff of breath rushing from between her parted lips.

"Avar..." She gripped my shoulder. "It's getting stronger."

"I know, sweetheart. But there is no need to worry. I'll stay with you until it passes."

The spell of the collar was made to last through an entire night. Maddy had been managing it amazingly well. I'd feared she'd be in distress or even in so much anguish that her mind might give in and break. Instead, she smiled and stretched like a kitten ready for petting when I placed her in my bed.

"It feels weird," she pondered. "I don't feel in control, which should be unnerving, but it's actually exciting. Maybe because I'm with you?"

Warmth pulsed deep in my chest at her words. I wished they meant that she felt trust and affection for me. But they meant nothing. Tonight, her words carried no lasting meaning. I had to remember that.

"It's the collar speaking instead of you," I reminded us both.

I needed this reminder, lest this warm, unfamiliar feeling would lead me astray. It wasn't *me* who made her lean into my touch and open her legs in invitation. It was Travan's cursed collar. I just happened to have a little more decency than the man who had put this collar on a woman the last time. I would not have forced her to wear it, but I proved rotten enough to enjoy seeing her whimpering and dripping with need.

"I want you, Avar," she moaned.

Heat throbbed through my entire being, burning like a lightning bolt in my crotch. Yet I forced it down, keeping my cock concealed. I couldn't fuck her. Not even when she begged me. Not even if the need burned me alive.

All I could do was touch her. There was no other way to help her without that. I slipped the tip of my right tentacle between her legs, my corollas kissing her skin on the way.

She opened wider for me.

"Please, Avar. I need you." She grabbed my hand and placed it on her breast.

I squeezed her breast lightly, stroking the hard bud of her nipple with my thumb. The sensation of her warm skin under my palm was exquisite, momentarily making me forget about anything else.

Impatient in her desperation, she slipped her hand between her legs, rubbing herself. Frustrated groans fell from her lips.

"You can't help yourself," I reminded her. "Let me do it for you."

Taking her hand in mine, I licked her fingers. Her flavor quickly proved addicting, and I couldn't get enough of it. Sliding a tentacle between her thighs, I placed a corolla over her most sensitive spot and wrapped it around it, like a rose petal around a pearl.

She gasped, bucking her hips. With my tentacle sucking at her on the outside, I slipped a finger inside her.

"It's so...so good." She rolled her head on the pillow, her eyes glazed over with lust. The pink glow of the collar made her skin look almost translucent. "More... I need more."

She turned to her side, then climbed to all fours.

"Fuck me, Avar. Please, I want you inside me." She thrust her plump, round bottom against my pelvis.

My cock sprang out against my will. With her eyes closed and her mind floating in the fog of lust, she didn't notice even as she thrust backwards against it.

My mind reeled as if under a spell too. An intense need for her surged through my very essence. It'd be so easy to slip inside her. My shaft was as thick as her thigh, but I could force it to shrink to fit her sweet, dripping hole perfectly. I could...

But Maddy wasn't herself. My cock, my finger, my tentacle —it was all the same to her right now. She wouldn't know how she really felt about any of it until the sun came up and the spell wore off. Until then, she was entirely at my mercy. She had no choice but to trust me. And I'd be worth less than the slime in a bog if I broke her trust. She'd hate me if I did, and I'd hate myself even more.

Instead of plunging inside her, I cupped her ass with my hand and carefully moved away the temptation. Reining in my aching cock, I slipped a tentacle around her thighs and gently stroked the slick heat between them.

She moaned in pleasure. Her elbows bucked, sending her into my sheets, with her delectable bottom sticking up in the air.

Oh, sweet temptation, who could escape you, be he a human or a sin?

Not me, clearly.

I plopped on my back, my feelers trembling in anticipation. I lifted Maddy over my head, careful not to hurt her with my horns.

"Avar? What are you doing?" she murmured, breathless from desire.

"I need another taste." I positioned her dripping slit over my mouth.

My feelers curled around her thighs, keeping her in place as I plunged my tongue inside her.

She squeaked, halting her breath at the invasion.

"Oh God, Avar, so good..." She rode my tongue, gripping my tentacles for support.

I sucked on the hot little bud of her clit. My feelers strayed all over her body, and I had to hold them back from exploring places she might not want me to explore if she wasn't wearing the cursed collar.

She tensed, rubbing herself faster against my mouth, then screamed, coming hard. Trembling, she fell forward, letting go of my tentacles and gripping my horns instead.

With her hot, little palms wrapped around my sensitive horns, desire shot through me like a lance of heat. I jerked with a violent shudder. Losing her balance, Maddy fell off my face and onto the covers. She stared at me, catching her breath.

Her gaze slid downwards, where my cock bobbed out in the open—thick, hard, and pulsing with desire to ravish her for the rest of the night and beyond.

"You do have a dick." Her throat bobbed with a swallow. "And what a marvelous one at that! It's simply fantastic, Avar, just like the rest of you."

I didn't know where I found the strength to pull my cock back in to hide it from view, but I did.

"Aww." Maddy pouted. "That's not fair. You've touched and licked me everywhere tonight. I want my turn to do it to you too."

"It's not about me." I slid my hand up her side, skimming her hip before cupping her breast.

It shouldn't be about me, but the pleasure I derived from touching her couldn't be helped. Her orgasms resonated through me with need I could barely control. I only hoped my self-restraint would last longer than the collar's spell.

"How are you feeling?" I palmed her breast, kneading it gently. With her mind lost to the spell, her attention turned back to her need once again.

"Better but..." She let her knees fall apart, opening for me. "It's not over yet."

"Are you ready for more? Or do you need a break?"

I pinched the hard bud of her nipple. Her hips jerked in response, and she whimpered.

"More, please. I'll rest after."

Lowering my head to her chest, I stroked and tweaked her nipples with my feelers while my hand slipped between her legs to play with her again.

It'd been a while since I had a soul in this bed. Maddy's sweet body was a special treat, of course. But nobody had ever enticed me this much before.

I'd been with a woman who was still in possession of her mortal body only once before. She was a nun in the monastery where I'd come to retrieve the recipe for the transcendence potion I had to replenish in order to travel between worlds. The moment after I'd made her come, the fun-loving but pious nun called me a demon and tried to stab me with her crucifix, forgetting all about how she'd begged me to fuck her just a minute earlier.

Humans were bizarre creatures. Their relationships tended to be messy. I loved pleasure, just like all my brothers did, but I wouldn't sacrifice my sanity for it. An occasional night with a soul stuck in Purgatory was good enough for me. A soul knew what it wanted. There was no need to pretend. A soul wouldn't beg me for sex, then try to send me to hell tormented by guilt right after.

I hoped Maddy wouldn't be wracked by guilt come morning, either. Whatever she felt tonight, I hoped she'd remember it fondly. Because I knew I would.

She climaxed again, with my name fluttering off her parted lips, her fingers fisted in the bedding.

"I don't know how much more I can take," she said softly, hiding her face in the sheets.

Sweat beaded between her shoulder blades. I pulled a blanket over her flushed, naked body.

"You should rest while you can. Close your eyes. I won't touch you unless you need me again."

She sighed, shifting closer.

"Who knew a mortal sin would be this considerate?" She smiled, her eyelids drooping already.

Lust must've taken a toll on her body. I didn't have a body, but I felt tired too. I promised not to touch her, but I stretched alongside her and let her snuggle into my chest.

"For the record," she murmured, her warm breath tangling with the feelers of my beard, "I don't find your tentacles repulsive. In some monstrous, terrifying way, I actually find you very attractive. You are a kind, handsome monster, Avar, and I like you very much."

It must be the effect of the collar's curse. She had far more reasons to hate me than to like me.

Yet her words made me feel warm inside. Somewhere, deep in my chest where humans had their hearts, I wished there was a way for her to truly like me, without the collar and its spell.

Exhausted, Maddy fell asleep within moments, snoring softly into my beard. She'd be awake soon, writhing and moaning with a new attack of need. The collar wouldn't let her rest for long until morning. And when it was over, she'd return to her own room again.

A sudden regret gripped me. For the first time in my never-ending life, I wouldn't mind sharing my bed for longer than just a night or two. Working side by side with her made my days that much brighter. Now I wished I could spend all my nights with her too.

I lifted a tentacle and ran it along Maddy's shape from her head down to her toes, hovering it just above her without touching. Every curve and every dip of her body belonged to me. I owned it. And tonight, I learned exactly how to use it to bring her pleasure. But it wasn't enough.

The problem with greed was that no matter how much I had, it was never enough.

Her body was mine. But I wanted more. Now, I needed to possess her soul too. Without a soul, the body was nothing but an empty shell, and I craved to own the light that breathed life into it, that made her sigh and laugh, walk and talk, glare at me or beg for my touch.

I wanted Maddy, both body and soul.

She spent the rest of the night alternating between drifting to sleep from exhaustion and begging for sex. Sometime after midnight, we ate the dinner that E had brought, then went back to bed. By morning, the spell had finally worn off, allowing us both to get some sleep.

I woke up to a slight tapping against one of my feelers. The bright sunlight flooded my cave through the skylights in the side of the mountain. Lying on her side, Maddy held my feeler in her fingers, examining it closely.

She noticed I was awake and quickly let go of the feeler.

"Morning." She smiled awkwardly. "Did I wake you up?"

"No," I lied, hiding a yawn in my beard. "I was almost awake anyway."

"I didn't know that sins slept. Come to think of it, there are so many things I still don't know about you."

"Is that why you were examining my feeler?"

She smiled again. "I was just trying to figure out how I could touch you when you're not supposed to have a body."

"I don't have a body in the way you do. There are no bones, tissue, or blood. But I am a being. I exist. I have a presence that may be more noticeable in some worlds than in others. In the human world, I'm more of an idea, considerably less defined or tangible than I am in Purgatory. Here, my presence is more solid, and so is my shape."

She ran a hand up my arm, then squeezed my shoulder.

"If it's not flesh and blood, then what is it?"

"Light and shadows. Color and scent. Not everything that lives is made of flesh and blood, my presumptuous little human." I slipped a finger under her chin and tilted her face up for a kiss.

She allowed me to guide her to my mouth. Her lips parted. Warmth throbbed in my chest with anticipation. The spell of the collar was now gone. Maddy truly wanted me to kiss her. And I wanted it more than anything in the world.

I spread my feelers, eager for our lips to touch.

But she jerked away, leaning back.

"I..." She blinked, glancing aside. "Thank you for your help last night. But we shouldn't..."

The shimmering bubble of hope in my chest burst to pieces and vanished. Grim reality settled back instead. I wasn't supposed to kiss Maddy, no matter how much I wanted it or how natural it felt to be with her.

Clearing my throat, I moved my finger to her necklace instead.

"How are you feeling this morning?"

She touched her neck, saying nothing.

With the curse being over, the collar now looked like a necklace once again. The stones separated into pink flowers inside the golden filigree setting.

"Do you want me to take it off?"

"Yes. Please." She shifted closer and tossed the tangled mane of her dark hair over her shoulder to expose the closure on the back of her neck. "Can you do it now?"

The closure proved too small for my fingers, but it opened under the tip of one of my feelers.

"There you go." I released her.

"Ooof." She rubbed her neck with relief, as if I'd taken the heavy boards of a medieval pillory from around it. "Thank you. What is this thing, anyway?" Maddy glowered at the collar in my hand. "Where did you get it?"

"It's a long story."

Using a tentacle, I placed the collar on the stone ledge that ran around the bed. I should return it to its box sooner rather than later, then lock the box in a safe place. But Maddy was still in my bed, and that was exactly where I wished to be, for as long as it lasted.

Thankfully, she didn't seem to be in a hurry to leave, either.

"We have some time, don't we? Tell me the story, even if it's a long one." She propped her head on her elbow, pulling the covers higher over her chest. "Tell me about the choker, please. Why do you have it?"

"This piece wasn't created with good intentions, Maddy."

"I gathered that much." A somber shadow crossed her lovely face. "Please tell me you weren't the one who created it."

"No. Absolutely not." I propped my head on an elbow, too, towering over her. To keep eye contact, she had to roll to her back, looking up. "The collar was made by a mage of Emperor Travan who gifted it to his concubine, Princess Pialeni."

"He *gifted* it to her? Did she ask for it? How did he have a princess for a concubine in the first place?"

"Princess Pialeni was the only daughter of Travan's sworn enemy. Travan and her father had fought a long and bloody war for over a decade when Travan's people captured Princess Pialeni on his orders. He intended to use her against her father but took a liking to her and quickly got obsessed. Unfortunately for him, the princess hated her captor with a passion that no lavish gifts could extinguish. Travan even offered to make her his wife, but the princess only laughed in his face. Infuriated, he forced her to become his lover."

"He forced her? Do you mean he raped her?" Maddy paled, but such was the bitter truth of their lives.

"Repeatedly." I nodded. "The power was on his side, there was nothing she could do. He brought her to his chambers almost nightly and had his way with her. Yet her spirit remained intact, and her hatred for him grew. With time, owning unwilling Pialeni's body was no longer enough for Travan. He wished for her to want him, too, to need him, and to beg him. So, he ordered his mage to make the collar using my brother's spell of lust. The wearer of the collar becomes overcome with passion but can't find release on their own, needing help from another."

She grimaced in disgust, peering through my chest at the collar on the ledge behind me. "Why did you even want that thing?"

I wondered how to explain my all-consuming need to possess and the excruciating fear of loss that came with it. Unique things were often fragile or small. And if a one-of-a-kind item broke or got misplaced, it'd be possibly lost forever.

"The collar was the only one made, and no other can ever be created again," I said. "When Lux, the Sin of Lust, learned about the collar, he changed the spell and has been keeping it a secret ever since."

"The Sin of Lust didn't condone the creation of that collar?"

"Of course not. Lust is the source of one of the world's biggest pleasures, but only as long as everyone is a willing participant. For the unwilling ones, the lust of others is torture, which is not what my brothers and I are about. We bring pleasure to those who sin with us. Anguish, despair, and sorrow are best left for the virtues. My sisters thrive on sacrifice."

Maddy bit her lip, a wrinkle of concentration forming between her dark eyebrows.

"Did you steal the collar from Princess Pialeni?" she asked.

Of course, she'd assume I stole everything, just like I'd stolen her.

"No. I *traded* with the princess. In exchange for the necklace, I gave her a dagger laced with poison. She killed Travan with it the very next night, then escaped his palace, and returned to her father's kingdom."

Maddy breathed a sigh of relief for the princess.

"Please tell me Travan is rotting in hell now."

I shook my head. "The Higher Judgment ruled otherwise for them. Both Travan and Pialeni have been sent back to their world several times now. In every lifetime, he finds her and begs her to be his. And every time, she refuses him."

"Is that fair? To use her as the tool for his punishment?"

"The Higher Judgment is infallible. The princess must have her own atonement to complete."

She scrambled into a sitting position. The cover fell to her lap, exposing her breasts. She quickly grabbed the blanket and covered them up, proving that the spell of the collar was truly gone. She no longer wanted me to see her naked.

A pang of regret squeezed my chest.

"But they don't remember their previous lives, do they?" she asked. "Pialeni and Travan can't recognize each other in every lifetime?"

"That's right, they can't. They meet as strangers. Yet his obsession with her and her hatred for him proved to be too large for one lifetime, spreading into all of them. Power has never been on his side again, however. He hasn't come close enough to even touch her. She has refused him over a dozen times now. So, in a way, he *is* in hell—only in the one of his own making."

She sat in silence for a few moments, probably pondering the wisdom and logic of the Higher Judgment.

"Do you agree with that?" she asked.

"What does it matter if I do or not? No one can change the verdict of the Higher Judgment. Not even a Deadly Sin."

8

Madison

"Are there any cookies left?" Avar asked after breakfast. "The ones you made last night?"

A few days have passed since the unfortunate incident with the cursed collar. We'd settled back into the routine of working in the cave together as things went back to normal. Or at least I pretended very hard that they did.

"Yes. Why?"

I wasn't big on baking, but Avar had been building me a huge kitchen with gorgeous stone counters and a massive shiny stove I wanted to test. He volunteered to help me make a dessert last night. The recipe for sugar cookies was one of those that I remembered by heart. It also required only a few simple ingredients that we happened to have on hand.

"I want some." He got up from the table.

We had breakfast in the round room on the top of the mountain. Despite the huge new kitchen, lots of space remained here for an eating area as well, and we'd been having

95

all our meals here lately. The heavy, solid table that Avar had here to tag and organize items for his collection served well as a dining table too. And the open patio provided the best views of the sunset after dinner.

"You'll have dessert after breakfast?" I smiled.

"Why not?" He shrugged.

I couldn't come up with a single reason why a deadly sin could not have a cookie whenever the hell he wished. So, I opened the cabinet next to the stove and took out the cookie jar.

"Why not?" I echoed, taking one for myself too.

His beard spread with a smile.

"These are so good." He took a cookie in each hand, then grabbed a few in his feelers and tentacles too. "For later," he explained.

I wasn't a pastry chef. Baking was never my strength. But sugar cookies were simple enough to make, and I loved that he enjoyed them so much.

"Haven't you had cookies before?" I asked as we walked down the path to the cave for another day of sorting out his treasures.

"Not the ones made by you." He glanced my way, stuffing another cookie in his mouth.

Something in his glance sent a warm blush to my cheeks.

Having Avar around had become as natural as breathing. When he stepped away even for a moment, I felt like an essential part I needed for comfort was missing. Maybe it had to do with his size and his larger-than-life presence that left an equally large void in his absence.

Something remained unspoken between us, however. And it had everything to do with that cursed night with the collar.

As I watched him shake the crumbs from his beard, I remembered how gently his feelers glided down my body when he kissed my breasts or dipped his tongue inside me. I never forgot how wonderful his hands felt on my skin or how tenderly his delicate corollas peppered me with kisses.

The memory of him trying to kiss me the morning after still filled me with regret that the kiss hadn't happened. I'd waited for it both with excitement and a little trepidation. But as he'd moved closer, a prudent thought that I shouldn't be kissing my abductor had stirred in my mind. Then his beard had moved, startling me, and I'd jerked away.

I didn't lie when I told him that his looks didn't repulse me. But his appearance was exceptionally unusual, requiring some time getting used to.

Now I wonder what kissing Avar would feel like.

He stopped abruptly, watching me closely.

"Maddy?" His voice came out rough but gentle. Prodding and hopeful.

At some point, he'd switched to calling me Maddy instead of Madison. I'd told him that the nickname was reserved for my friends. Clearly, he must consider us friends now. But I didn't know how to put into words everything that I felt. Also, I wasn't sure if I should be putting it into words at all. Instead of confessing my feelings to the sin who held me captive, shouldn't I do my best to try getting over them?

Freeing my gaze from his, I glanced over his shoulder into the green valley below the mountain.

"It's a beautiful day today," I said, in a desperate attempt to change the subject. "Can we take a break from working in the cage today?"

Today, I'd rather avoid working in close proximity with the mortal sin who became increasingly more attractive to me the more time we spent together.

"What would you like to do instead?" he asked.

"Go outside, maybe? For a walk? Or shopping? I could use a few things to make dinner tonight."

E had been bringing me ingredients along with food from Gul. I'd been making our lunches for the past few days, but I could certainly do more than that. I missed cooking.

"Can we go to the market in town?" I asked. "E mentioned there is one."

"There is. Right."

"Great. I can make us dinner tonight. A curry, maybe? But I'd like to get some fresh herbs for it. Or I could make some tacos," I added excitedly. "Have you had tacos before?"

"I'm not sure." Avar proceeded down the path. "But I'll eat anything you make."

The sins, just like souls, didn't need food for sustenance. But Avar had gotten into the habit of sharing all my meals with me, even the morning coffee.

"I'll take you to the market," he said.

"Or I could go on my own and just ask someone in town where it is."

His beard shifted as he mulled over my suggestion.

"You don't want me to come along?"

"I didn't say that." I wasn't against Avar coming with me. In fact, I preferred his company. But I wanted to see if he'd let me go on my own. "You could stay and work here while I'm gone, get some things done."

He peered at me closely.

"We can get things done together later. What I need to hear from you now is the truth, Maddy. Do you want me to come along or not?"

Well, if it was the truth that he wanted...

"I want to know if you'll let me go alone. Can you let go of me even for a few hours? Or will I have to spend the rest of my life glued to your hip?"

He stepped back, leaning against the mountain wall. The path stopped moving as we stared each other down.

"Giving you space doesn't mean letting go of you," he said. "You're mine, no matter where you are. If your soul needs some time for itself—as many souls do—you can very well take a walk alone." He gave me a tight smile.

His posture remained relaxed against the rock wall. But his tentacles went unnaturally still. Even the feelers in his beard stiffened as if every word he said pained him.

It was incredibly hard for Avar, the Sin of Greed, to let go of anything he considered his, including me. Now that I got to know him a little better, I suspected it cost him a huge effort to let me out of his sight even for a moment, but I appreciated the effort.

"All right, so then—" I started.

He lifted his hands up, fingers splayed. His feelers flared out too.

"Just...be careful. Please," he said with force.

"What is so dangerous in Purgatory?"

"Not dangerous. Just..." He pinched the bridge of his nose. "Don't talk to anyone you don't know, aside from the souls at the market, of course. Especially if you run into any of my brothers."

"Well, if I meet Gul or Sup, I should at least thank them for the food and clothes, don't you think? And the others—"

"*Don't* talk to the others. If it's Lux... Uhgr," he groaned. "Stay away from Lux. And Invi..." He scraped his hand down his face. "If you see Invi, Maddy, just run away from him as fast as you can."

"Is he that bad?"

"Not bad but maddening. He'd take you just to vex me. I'd get you back, of course, one way or another. But neither you nor I need that aggravation."

He paced the path back and forth. His tentacles undulated restlessly, as he tried to foresee every "aggravation" real and imagined that I could possibly encounter while out there on my own.

"Stay on the main road all the way to the town. When you get to the teahouse, ask a soul for the directions to the market. It's pretty straightforward from there. Don't let the merchants drag you into lengthy conversations. Some souls really like to talk. I trust your judgment, but souls change here often. One can never know what new ones are like that arrive here every day."

"Avar." I went for his hand but missed it and grabbed the tip of his tentacle instead, then squeezed it gently. "It's okay. You can come with me if you want."

He spun around, facing me. "Really? You don't mind?"

"I would love for you to come this time. But it's also good to know that I can leave the mountain and go for a walk on my own if I feel like it."

"Well, you're a free soul. You should be able to come and go as you please," he said hesitantly, as if trying to get used to the idea. "As long as you come back, of course."

"And stay away from Lux and Invi, and all the souls who talk too much." I smiled.

He caught on with my teasing tone and matched it. "And everyone else, really." He exhaled a long breath of relief and wound both his tentacles around me. "Just stay with me, Maddy." He lifted me into his embrace, bringing me up to his level. "Just like this."

"Just like this." I cupped his face. His feelers spiraled up my arms. His eye color warmed from deep purple to a gentle violet.

For that one moment, I really didn't wish to be anywhere else but *just like this*.

The market in Purgatory lay outside of the town's center, taking up an area almost as big as the town itself. The wide aisles ran up and between the surrounding hills. The merchants' stands boasted bright canvas canopies of patterns that seemed to have come from all over the world and beyond.

Souls didn't *need* anything to survive, therefore the wares in Purgatory market were only the items that someone might *want*. Everything on display was either meant to bring pleasure to the buyer or had already brought pleasure to its creator, who had made it and was now selling it. Often, it was both.

Rows of stands held all possible kinds of artisan creations—knits, paintings, ceramics, jewelry, tiny figurines, giant carvings, and things I wasn't even sure what they were other than the artist must've enjoyed making them.

"Food is that way." Avar pointed to the right.

The moment we'd merged with the crowds browsing the aisles, his right tentacle formed a protective loop around me. He didn't quite hug me with it, keeping it wide enough for me to walk inside it. But no one could bump into me or even come close enough to touch.

The souls strolled by, paying little attention to Avar, who towered above all of us. However, the moment they spotted me, they'd often do a double-take, or even stop and openly gape at me. Having Avar close made me feel both physically and emotionally supported in the crowd.

Just like the rest of the market, the food stands held little of what would be considered staple items or necessities back in my old world. I didn't see anyone selling milk, eggs, or sacks of grains. But there was an entire aisle of pastries and elaborately decorated cupcakes. A whole row of stands displayed curried meats and cold cuts, thinly sliced and rolled into visually stunning flowers and rosettes. There were fruit bouquets, and chocolate sculptures, and spun sugar figurines, making the food aisles resemble an art exhibition.

The other thing I noticed that made this market different from any other I'd ever visited back home was the small quantity of products being sold. Most merchants only had one tray of cupcakes, each differently decorated; or a basket of pastries, each of a different kind; or a single platter of fruit. There was no need to produce or sell a lot. Everyone made only as much or as little as they enjoyed making it.

And of course, no money was exchanged. During our walk down here, Avar had explained to me that after their arrival in Purgatory, many souls still found comfort in the familiar routine of having an occupation. They returned to something they enjoyed in their past life or picked up a new activity that they couldn't do back in our world. The souls baked, or painted, or sang on the town square. Some enjoyed gardening, cooking, or painting. They then brought the fruits of their creative labor to the market.

I spotted the herb I needed on a silver tray in one of the stands.

"Is this cilantro?"

"Indeed, it is." The soul selling it beamed. "I found it over there behind that hill. There is a lot growing there. Smell it. Doesn't it smell nice?"

I picked up the small bundle and took a sniff.

"It is nice. What do you want for it?"

The soul shrugged. "I'll take a smile, if you feel like smiling this fine morning."

"I do. I have some very good reasons to smile today. It's a beautiful day, and I just found cilantro in Purgatory." I grinned, putting the herb into the basket we'd brought with us. "Thank you."

As we walked away from the stand, I tugged Avar's tentacle for him to bend down to me.

"What a steal, isn't it?" I whispered excitedly. "I knew souls didn't trade in money. But I only just realized that I could afford everything here. Absolutely everything."

Avar didn't seem as excited as I felt.

"Your smile is worth far more than a bunch of herbs, if you ask me."

"I have lots of smiles, dear Avar. Here," I grinned at him. "Have one for free. My gift."

He shook his head.

"That smile, Maddy, it's one of the biggest treasures in this world. Don't sell it short."

He held my gaze as his beard moved, his feelers spreading in that particular way they did when he smiled. It reflected in his eyes, too, making them sparkle with warmth and humor.

I wondered how much *his* smile would go for and how much I personally would give just to see it every day.

The air seemed to heat up around us as our gazes connected. Unable to stand the intensity, I glanced away and grabbed the first fruit I saw from the closest stand. It was a plump, purple grape, so big, I could barely eat it in one bite.

"Hey!" the seller yelled, making me jump. "You haven't paid for that."

"Sorry," I said around the mouthful of the juicy grape. It wasn't like I could spit it out and return it now. "What do you want for it?"

"I sell them for conversations, but now I'm not sure if I even want to talk to you at all."

Avar moved forward menacingly. I squeezed his tentacle, holding him back. There was no need for him to fight my battles. Especially since there was no battle at all. It was just a misunderstanding. I felt stupid for grabbing something without asking first, even if it was just a grape not sold for money.

"I'll gladly talk to you," I said sweetly, trying to pacify the grumpy soul.

Sulking, it didn't reply to my gesture of goodwill. The colors within its frame undulated in swirls, ranging from dark blue to silver-gray, and I wondered if that was the sign of the soul being annoyed with me.

"What's your name?" I tried my best to salvage the situation.

"I don't have one."

"All right. Do you go by he, she, or anything else?" It wasn't easy to tell by the soul's appearance. Either way, appearances were often deceiving.

The soul considered my question for a few moments.

"He. I was a man in my past life," he finally said with certainty.

His tone remained displeased, but at least he was talking to me.

"I'm very sorry I took your grape. I was distracted..." I let my voice trail off, not wishing to shift the blame on Avar now. It wasn't his fault that I found everything about him so fascinatingly distracting.

"Do you think it's forgivable to take things that don't belong to you?" the vendor asked.

"I think most sins should be forgivable, yes. As long as one genuinely regrets the wrong they have done. This is what this place is all about, isn't it? To cleanse one of their sins?"

"Purgatory for everyone is what they make it to be," the soul replied quizzically, then added unexpectedly, "I used to take what wasn't mine too. A lot. Do you think the circumstances in which the crime was committed can make it either more or less forgivable?"

I considered my answer carefully.

"I would think so, yes."

"Like, would it matter what I took and who I took it for?"

"Probably," I replied, somewhat uncertain. It was hard to pass judgment on a situation I knew so little about because I had a feeling he was not talking about the grapes.

He stared at the tray with the remaining fruit.

"I forgive you," he said somberly.

"Thank you." I lingered by his stand, unsure if our short conversation was enough for the grape to be considered paid for now. Our exchange felt a little odd, but it seemed to make sense to this soul.

"Maybe that's what I have to figure out now?" he mumbled to himself. "The ratio of guilt to the pleasure of possession where the value of what's stolen is determined by the individual need of each party. If I solve the equation and find the balance, then maybe I'd be able to move on?"

It sounded like a rhetorical question to me, but he seemed hopeful, like he had stumbled upon something important.

"Well, good luck," I wished him sincerely. "And thanks for the grape."

He perked up as I moved past his stall.

"Wait!" He caught up with me. "This was worth much more than one grape. Here." He shoved the entire tray in my hands. "Take it. I hope you'll enjoy it."

"Um...thank you. I will."

I turned to Avar. He silently moved our basket closer for me to put the fruit in. The transaction between the soul and me seemed to make sense to him. So, I accepted the grapes and thanked the soul again before moving ahead.

We picked up a few more items. But I quickly realized that

even in the market that demanded no money, there were still prices I couldn't pay. Frank, genuine conversations took time and an emotional toll. Most vendors also refused to accept fake smiles, but genuine ones proved harder to muster the more tired I grew.

Thankfully, there wasn't anything else I needed.

"We can go home," I said to Avar when we reached the end of an aisle.

He nodded, leading me back toward the town. As we came to the main road, a familiar voice called from up ahead.

"Madison!" E rushed to me. Slipping under the protective hoop of Avar's tentacle around me, she grabbed me into a hug. "I'm leaving Purgatory! Can you believe it?"

"Where are you going?"

"Back to Earth." She beamed. "The Higher Judgment has finally been made for me."

"You're to return to Earth?" I asked carefully.

To my knowledge, E's goal had been to enter a paradise, which wasn't what she got. But she seemed excited, and I didn't want to dampen her enthusiasm.

"Yes. I'm finally moving on. And this time, it'll be totally different. I was told I'll be born into a filthy rich family. Fast cars, huge mansions, amazing parties. I'll have it all! It'll be so much fun. I can't wait. I'm so glad I ran into you before leaving. I went to the mountain, but you weren't there, and I wanted to say goodbye."

"Thank you for finding me. I'm really happy for you, E. Enjoy your life. I'll see you again but hopefully not too soon?"

"Maybe I'll see you straight up *there* next time?" She laughed happily, pointing up at the sky. "This has got to be my last life on Earth, I can feel it. And what a life it would be. I'm going to have my own private jet!"

Avar swept aside his tentacle, and E headed along the road

that led to the Gates she had to go through to start her fifteenth lifetime in our world.

"Bye, Avar!" She waved, grinning over her shoulder. "I hope I'll never see you again. No offense."

"None taken." He used both his right hand and right tentacle to wave her goodbye.

I watched E skipping along the road and tried to feel happy for her, but I feared she was excited for all the wrong reasons.

"She'll be back to Purgatory, won't she?" I asked Avar.

He nodded confidently. "We'll definitely see her here again."

E was a restless soul. She craved adventure, excitement, and fun. Purgatory, with its small-town feel, where everything seemed to be suspended in waiting for something, wasn't the ideal place for someone like her.

Or maybe that merchant at the market was right when he said that Purgatory was what one made of it. For E, it had always been just a place of transit. She was happy to move on, even if the destination wasn't exactly what she had wished for.

As we passed the teahouse, I spotted Charity in her usual place at the table with a teacup in her hand.

"Good morning." I waved at her.

She gave me a tight smile and a small wave but didn't invite me to have tea with her this time. I caught the glare she tossed at Avar. He grunted, promptly walking away.

"You don't get along with your sister at all, do you?" I stated the obvious.

"We're polar opposite. Charity disapproves of anything I am. If she had it her way, she'd let me die, then celebrate my demise with glee." He shrugged. "It's hard to love someone like that, even if we are related."

Would the world be a better place without Avar, like Charity believed? A little while ago, I would've said yes with no hesitation. Now, just imagining him gone filled me with profound sadness.

"Souls can't die but sins can?" I asked.

"We can cease to exist, yes. Many people would welcome that."

"It's because they think you're part of the evil that plagues this planet."

He lowered his head, catching my upward glance. "What do *you* think?"

"I believe there is good in you," I spoke from the heart. "Maybe if you acted on that good, you'll prove to the world you aren't evil? There are many sides to you. Show them the side they have never seen."

"Which side is it, my little treasure? And how do you want me to show it?"

"Give back to humanity what you've taken from it."

"The very act of giving would kill me, Maddy, and I'm not virtuous enough to die for the greater good. I want to live."

How could I fault him for that? I didn't want to die either, even temporarily. I kept holding on to my body with everything I had.

"But could you not share even a little bit?" I wondered. "Or maybe *lend* things for people to use? There is so much good that could be done back home with what you have."

He heaved a long breath as we started our ascent along the path up the mountain.

"Many of my treasures could just as easily be used for evil as for good. Also, what if they got destroyed after leaving the safety of my mountain?"

"But why would anyone destroy things so valuable?"

I tried to climb over a root growing across the path. Wrapping his tentacle around my middle, Avar lifted me over it.

"Because that's what people do, Maddy. Humans tend to

ruin everything they touch, even the things they value the most. Do you know why I came to your world the night I took you?"

"To wreak havoc?" I offered with a teasing smile.

Technically, Avar remained my kidnapper and Purgatory was a trap, but I no longer thought about it with as much bitterness as I used to.

"Humans are good at wreaking havoc on their own," he retorted. "That night, I came to save a priceless piece of research that had been tossed into the garbage."

"You said the professor's ex-wife threw it away. Why would she do that if it was so valuable?"

"Out of lack of appreciation, of course." Avar scoffed. "Professor Lozhkin was a genius, though somewhat guilty of vanity. Since his previous research was stolen and the credit for most of his work went to someone else, he rigorously guarded his new project. No one knew what he was working on. He didn't have a single assistant and did everything on his own. When he suddenly passed away from a heart attack, there was no one to take over. His ex-wife inherited the apartment where he lived. She cleaned it, and all his priceless work ended up in the dumpster behind the building with the professor's apartment. That night, I mistook you for her. I thought you were bringing more of the professor's stuff to throw out."

Had I come out into the alley a little earlier or a little later than I did, I would've never come to Purgatory. Would I have been happier if I'd never met Avar?

Again, just a little while ago, my answer would've been a resounding yes. Now, I wasn't so sure. The mere thought of possibly never knowing his glowing presence, his rare hidden smiles, and the warm, supporting hugs filled me with sadness.

"What was Professor Lozhkin working on when he died?" I asked.

"An exoskeleton that would allow people with spinal cord

injuries to walk, run, and do a lot of other things as good or even better than they did before the injury."

"Really?" I gaped at him. "Was the device any good? Would his invention actually work?"

"It wasn't just a device, Maddy. Professor Lozhkin created a complex system that combined mechanics, electronics, and medication regimen. It was a work in progress, but he was on the right track with his research. It could work. As it often happens in human history, however, his genius work ended up in the dumpster. I saved it. And now, it's mine."

"Surely, it was a misunderstanding," I protested. "It ended up in the dumpster by mistake. The professor's wife didn't know or didn't understand—"

"I don't think it would've made any difference if she knew. The woman was set to destroy every shred of his legacy. I have a good reason to believe she was instrumental in his death too."

"Where is Professor Lozhkin now? Is he here?"

"Not anymore. He departed for a paradise of his choosing. But his isn't an isolated case. Humans can't always be trusted with valuable, irreplaceable treasures. Most of the things in my collection wouldn't exist if it wasn't for me. My one regret is that even I can't save it all. I only managed to get about half of the scrolls from the burned warehouse of the Library in Alexandria. The rest perished in the fire and can never be recovered. However, if I left it up to humans, all the forty thousand scrolls would've been gone."

"Wait a minute." I stopped him, my mind reeling. "Did you just say you saved some writings from the Library of Alexandria?"

He nodded somberly. "I got to the warehouse early enough, just after the docks caught on fire. But I still failed to save it all."

"Do you realize what that means?" I gestured for him to bend down to me, needing to see his face closer. Instead, he lifted me to him, settling me in the crook of his bent arm. I took his face between my hands and brought it to mine. "Can you imagine how much people could learn from the works that you saved?"

"Sadly, humanity doesn't learn much, and what little they do learn, they tend to forget quickly." Just like his words, his eyes held little faith in my kind. "Humans go back and forth in circles. You have no idea how frustrating it is to watch them stumbling around for so many centuries."

From what I knew about human history, his frustration was warranted. But Avar hadn't just been watching us "stumble around in circles," he tried to make a difference by saving and keeping what would've been otherwise irrecoverably lost.

"So all this time, you've been trying to preserve what we've been destroying?"

There were many aspects to greed, just as there were many sides to Avar. It thrilled me to discover all the new facets of his personality. I enjoyed the process of getting to know him so much, I almost didn't notice how much closer every discovery brought me to him.

Madison

"*This could be a good life for me here in Purgatory,*" I thought, watching Avar getting tea ready in our favorite room on top of the mountain.

I made sandwiches for lunch while he washed the fruit from the market and set the table.

"Why don't we take the afternoon off too?" he suggested.

With Avar being so much bigger than me, his furniture was also scaled to his size, making me feel like a doll. I climbed into the chair and had to fold my legs under me to sit at the table at the appropriate height.

"To do what?" I asked.

"We can stay here. I have to organize my records, and you can read your book. Judging by the clouds, the sunset will be lovely tonight."

He poured the tea in my cup, and I smiled as his tentacle stroked my knee under the table.

"Taking a day off sounds great." I covered his hand on the table with mine.

Avar turned his hand, catching mine in his palm. His fingers curled around my hand, cradling it.

"Touching you is one of the most exquisite pleasures I've ever felt." He stroked his thumb over my hand. "What do you feel when I touch you, Maddy?"

I shifted forward on my chair. I should say nothing, but some feelings are so hard to contain. My chest overflowed with emotions, and the words rushed out.

"Well, that night," I said, "when I was wearing the collar, do you remember how I acted and what I did?"

His eyes darkened to deep purple. "How could I ever forget?"

"Well, not all of that was because of the collar," I confessed. "I enjoy your touch, too, Avar."

He groaned. "Come here."

Reaching over the table with both tentacles, he snatched me from my chair and hauled me into his lap.

"I don't think I'll let you read any books today," he growled softly.

He kissed the side of my neck, his feelers slipping into the neckline of my dress.

I breathed faster. "I don't think I want to keep reading that book, anyway."

"You don't like it?" He kissed my shoulder, sliding the fabric of my dress down. "Heavens and hell," he groaned softly against my skin. "I wanted to do this to you again so badly."

Warm tingles scattered along my skin from where his feelers caressed and stroked. They skimmed my breasts just above the edge of my bra. I wished they'd slide in deeper, and I hoped they wouldn't at the same time.

Without the collar, my actions were all my own. If I let it go any further, I'd have no one to blame but myself.

Only how far was too far?

In my mind, I knew I probably shouldn't allow any of it.

"The book..." I used our conversation like a lifesaver. "I'm not sure what to say about it, really. The story started out interestingly enough, but the prose is so tedious. The descriptions are insanely long. For example, Evior, the author, describes a random old chair in every detail for an entire paragraph, then doesn't even end up sitting in it."

He held me tightly, nuzzling my shoulder, but didn't go any further, as if sensing my hesitation.

"As a child, Evior was an apprentice of a historical record keeper for a High Lord in Nerifir," he said. "He was trained to record every mundane detail of the High Lord's life."

"That explains it. Except that when he talks about something that seems to be super important, he doesn't describe it at all. He goes on and on about how this rare precious thing he made is the only one in existence and how kings would give up their kingdoms to get their hands on it, but he doesn't even mention what that thing looks like."

"What thing?" Avar lifted his head from my shoulder.

Not willing to let go of him yet, I trapped one of his feelers in my hand, then curled its tip around my finger.

"He calls it 'horologe,' which is like a watch, right? Except that instead of telling time, it controls it when one travels across the River of Mists."

Avar's features pinched in concentration as I spoke. He leaned closer, as if not to miss a single word.

"What did you just say? A horologe?"

"Yes." I blinked under his intense stare. "Apparently, there is an issue when one crosses the river that connects all the worlds, including Nerifir and our human world. Evior says in the book one can never know what time one would arrive when leaving a world for another. They can end up centuries ahead or years before the time when they left."

"From what I've read about the River of Mists, that is true. The river loops and twists between the worlds, making it nearly impossible to return to the same time you left from."

"Have you ever been to Nerifir yourself?"

"No. But I have found a few items from it in your world. As I said before, those from Nerifir have been crossing the river every now and then, despite the time leap. But I've never heard of a device that controls time."

"Evior says he built it by using the magic of a werewolf goddess."

His frown deepened.

"Ghata?"

"Yes. You know her?"

"Not personally, thankfully. But I've heard of her. She was the embodiment of the Moon Goddess. The werewolves of the Kingdom of Sarnala in Nerifir used magic to grant a physical body to their beloved goddess so she could live among them. Sadly, things didn't go well, as it often happens when deities mingle with mortals. The goddess became corrupted with the unlimited power over her subjects and ended up abusing the very people she was meant to protect."

"The book says that Evior escaped Nerifir because of her," I said. "She demanded he become her *brack*, which is like her monk or servant. So, his father found a portal to our world and sent him there for safety."

"It's a good thing he did. Ghata's *bracks* lost their free will and became her slaves in mind, body, and soul."

A shudder ran along my spine. Evior didn't have a single

good word to say about the goddess. It'd be a terrible fate to become her slave for life.

"In the book," I continued, "it's said that Ghata used her powers to send her *bracks* back and forth across the River of Mists multiple times, always bringing them back to her with no time leap issues. Evior then figured out how to harvest her moon powers and lock them in that horologe thingy. That's when I stopped reading as he went on and on about the mechanics of how it all works, using a lot of words I've never heard before. I fell asleep while reading and never picked it up again. Maybe I should just skip a few chapters and see if it gets better later? Some scenes from Nerifir were neat to read, like his family history and the description of the place where they lived."

Avar got up from the table with me in his arms.

"Did he write anything about where he stored the horologe?" He paced the room.

"Oh, I didn't make it that far in the book. Why?"

He kept pacing back and forth, turning so swiftly, my head started to spin.

I squirmed in his arms. "Can you set me down, please? I'm getting dizzy here."

"Sorry." He returned me to my chair. Gripping the back of the chair on each side of me, he leaned down to me. "Maddy, I really need to read that book."

The tacos turned out pretty good. I had two. Avar had none. The food on his plate was slowly turning cold as he kept reading the book he'd started before I even began making dinner.

"It's in Nerifir," he said, setting the book aside.

"Are you talking about that watch thingy?" I asked from across the table.

"Yes. Horologe. Evior brought it back to Nerifir, afraid that Ghata's magic would lead her to him. He wrote the book because he wanted people to know about his genius. Then he tried to burn it because he was afraid that someone would actually read it." Avar shook his head. "This man lived his entire life in fear, despite his greatness."

"Have you met him? Did he come to Purgatory?"

"No. He couldn't come here. Evior was a werewolf. His people have different beliefs about the afterlife, and our Purgatory isn't a part of it."

"It makes sense." I eyed the tacos on his plate. "So, are you going to eat those or...?"

"You can have them," he said, glancing back at the book. His mind seemed to drift far away from the food, from this room, and even from Purgatory.

"You want that thing, don't you? The horologe?" I took a bite of one of his tacos.

"I do. You have no idea how much, Maddy."

"Oh, I do have *some* idea about how badly you can want something. Or someone," I assured him.

He smirked into his beard, but didn't defend his abducting me.

"Evior is right," he said. "He could get a king's ransom for his device. Many in Nerifir would want the horologe that gives power over the unruly River of Mists."

"What would you do if you had it? How would you use it?"

"I'd use it to return from Nerifir without losing any time."

"And then?"

"Then, I would keep it here safely."

I huffed, disappointed. "But that'd be a waste of all its power."

"It'd be safer that way. The worlds connected by the River of Mists are not supposed to intermingle freely. The horologe makes it way too easy to travel between them, which can bring all possible kinds of troubles. The best place for it is in my collection."

I finished one of his tacos and took the other one. Clearly, his mind was not on the food tonight. It was a good thing he didn't need to eat to survive.

"When will you go?"

He raked his hands over his temples, then laced his fingers behind his head, staring straight ahead.

"I can't go." He exhaled slowly.

"What? Why not? I'll look after this place in your absence, if that's your worry. I promise not to touch anything and definitely not to try anything on anymore."

He smiled, probably remembering the collar.

"I trust you, Maddy, but I can't go to Nerifir. I mean, I can, but I won't be able to bring anything back, including the horologe."

"Why not?"

"In this world, humans or their souls believe in my existence, which gives me my form." He lifted a tentacle in demonstration of his tangible state. "In Nerifir, I'd be nothing but an apparition, unable to touch, to lift, or to carry anything, no matter how small. The few things I have from Nerifir, including this book, I acquired from your world, after someone else had brought them there, not by getting them from Nerifir myself."

"Well, that sucks. I'm really sorry, Avar."

He must feel terrible to discover something special only to realize that he couldn't have it.

I finished eating and took the plate to the sink while a thought churned in my mind.

"Are there humans in Nerifir?" I asked.

"None are born there. But there have been a few who have come from your world. There have even been a few human queens."

I turned around to face him, wondering if he realized the same thing I did.

"I could go to Nerifir instead of you then. Since I have a body, I'll be able to lift and carry things, including the horologe."

"No." He shook his head adamantly. "Every full moon, the werewolves turn into monsters with claws that would tear you to shreds and with teeth that drip poison."

Fear slithered down my spine as I imagined running into a beast like that, but I ignored it the best I could.

"I'll just have to go there during the day, then, or on any night other than the full moon."

"Without the horologe," he argued, "it's impossible to choose or even predict the time of day one would land after crossing the River of Mists."

I thought about that for a moment.

"But the full moon happens only once in twenty-eight days. The chance of me landing on any other day is much greater. Where is that thing, anyway? How long do I have to stay in Nerifir to find it?"

"Evior says he left it in care of a trusted keeper in a women's monastery that is located on the shore next to the portal."

"So, I'd just have to go on a short walk to the monastery and sweet-talk a nun into giving up her timepiece. That doesn't sound like a dangerous mission at all."

He came closer and crouched down to my eye level. Smiling, I put my hands on his wide shoulders.

"You want that horologe, Avar. Badly." It wasn't a question. I knew he did.

"More than anything..." He inhaled, then corrected himself, holding my gaze, "*Almost* more than anything in the world."

This was my chance, my one and only chance to make it right between us.

"You make deals, Avar, don't you? That's how you've acquired some things for your collection, including that cursed collar. The only way you can give something up is to trade it for something else."

"What are you saying, Maddy?" He sounded wary.

My heart pounded hard. I fisted my sweaty hands on his shoulders.

"Make a deal with me. I'll go to Nerifir and get the horologe that you want so much. And in exchange, you'll let me go. Let's trade my freedom for that precious relic."

He flinched as if I'd slapped him.

"Maddy, I can't lose you."

"But it'll be a trade, Avar. Not a loss."

His beard moved as he flexed his jaw. His eyes searched mine.

"Why, sweetheart?" he asked so tenderly, my heart all but broke. "Do you hate it here so much? Do you not like being with me?"

"No, it's not that, please..." I tried to soothe him.

"Tell me how I can make your life here better? I'll do anything to make you happy." He seemed to forget about the horologe already, reaching for me. "Do you still hate me for bringing you here?"

"I can't hate you, Avar. Not anymore. Not even if I tried."

When it came to him, I faced a much stronger emotion than hate. I feared I could fall in love with him.

"I wish things were different between us," I said. "I enjoy being with you, and I wish I could do that without reservations. But... How can I, if no matter what, you remain my captor?"

"A captor?"

He looked as if every word of mine was a stab of a dagger. It pained me to hurt him. But our truth was ugly, whether I spoke about it or not.

"I'm here because of you," I said. "Against my will. With no way out. Purgatory is lovely. But it's still a prison I cannot leave unless you release me. Please, let me go," I implored. "Set me free. Become my rescuer instead of my jailer, Avar. Make this deal with me."

He gripped the granite support of the sink behind me, caging me with his arms as if someone was about to whisk me away from him already.

"A deal would only work if what I got was of a higher value to me than what I gave up. But there simply is nothing more precious to me than you, Maddy."

His heartfelt confession should've made me happy. Anyone would want to be treasured as much as I knew Avar treasured me. But the word "precious" brought to mind his collection of rare, beautiful, priceless things. And I felt like a *thing,* too, the thing that didn't get locked up in a cabinet only because I proved to be more "amusing" outside of the glass box.

I already cared about Avar too much to be content with the role of one of his precious relics.

To stay with the man I was falling for, to keep him happy, I had to give up so many important parts of myself—my family, my friends, my life's purpose, my very life as I knew it. What would be left of me without all of that? I deserved better. Avar deserved more. A true relationship could never work like this.

Yet seeing his crestfallen expression was simply gut-wrenching.

"Maddy," he said softly, swiping a tear from my cheek I didn't know I'd spilled. "Nothing is worth *this*." He stared at my tear glistening on the tip of his finger.

I sniffled, wiping my cheeks with both hands.

He got up, straightening to his full, impressive height.

"I'll have my horologe," he said firmly. "You'll have your freedom. We have a deal."

10

Madison

In the end, Avar chose the relic over me. My gamble had paid off, and freedom was no longer a thing of the past. All I had to do now was to get that horologe for him. Then I would go back to my old life in my old world, where I belonged.

All the pieces would fall back into place again, and the restlessness inside me would finally be gone. Hopefully.

"When do you want me to go to Nerifir?" I asked Avar after the table had been cleared and the dishes had been washed. "Should I go now? I mean, why wait, right?"

"Now?" His eyebrows shot up to his horns. "But it's almost night already."

"From what I understand, time doesn't remain the same when one travels across the River of Mists. So, it doesn't matter when I leave here."

He hesitated. "But it's late. Aren't you tired?"

I tossed the dishcloth into the sink. "The sooner I go, the sooner it'll be over."

He leaned back against the table, his hands gripping the edge of the tabletop.

"So impatient to leave here, are you? To leave *me*." The wistful note in his voice was like a punch to my stomach.

I knew I had to leave Purgatory. My life back in my world wasn't over yet. It just got interrupted, and I had to do everything I could to put it back on track. But the truth proved impossible to hold back.

"I'll miss you," I admitted.

He gripped the table so hard, the wood cracked. Reaching for me with his tentacles, he pulled me closer. I stretched my arms up to him, and he lifted me into a hug.

I wrapped my arms around his neck, no longer caring if it was proper and no longer wondering how I should act. I'd be leaving soon. What did it matter if I told him the truth?

"I'll miss you terribly, Avar. I know that already."

The fresh evening breeze brought in the scent of lilacs from the patio, and I knew I was going to miss that scent too.

Raking my fingers through the feelers of his beard, I slid my hands up his cheeks and stroked the high ridges of his cheekbones with my thumbs.

His tentacles tightened around me. The feelers circled my wrists, trapping me.

Was it really a trap? Or a passionate embrace?

Should I try to get free? Or hold on tighter?

The feelers of his beard shrank suddenly. They grew shorter until they completely disappeared, leaving him with a clean-shaven look. I stroked along his strong jawline, learning the unfamiliar features that had been hidden from view by his beard.

"You are so heartbreakingly handsome," I said. "But you

don't need to hide the feelers from me. You don't ever need to hide any part of you from me, Avar."

With a breath of relief from him, his feelers extended again.

"Maddy, *my* Maddy," he repeated like a prayer under his breath. "I absolutely should *not* kiss you right now."

"It'd be wrong," I agreed, drawing him closer.

"Worse than wrong," he murmured against my lips, with the sweet flavor of grapes on his breath. "It'd be stupid, self-destructive..."

"Irresponsible," I echoed just before our mouths collided.

He groaned, his embrace tightening. My breath hitched. The kiss was all the things we'd said. It was stupid, self-destructive, and extremely irresponsible, considering the circumstances, but it didn't feel wrong. It felt more right than anything in the world.

Without the spell of the collar pushing me into his arms, the need for him grew subtly. Unlike the desperate passion that had overpowered everything then, I was able to savor every sensation now.

As his mouth claimed mine in a hungry kiss, the delicate corollas of his tentacles peppered my arms with far gentler kisses. The feelers of his beard caressed my neck softly. Pleasure rippled down my skin.

He might look like a monster, but wasn't it in human nature to be drawn to sin? For me, the pull to Avar proved irresistible. And just this once, I didn't wish to fight it.

As he leaned with his backside on the table, I stood on his thighs. Desire curled through me like a wisp of mist, growing stronger with his every caress.

A tentacle slipped under the shoulder strap of my dress. I moved my arm, letting the dress slide off. The feelers of his beard pushed the dress further down, caressing my chest. Curling around my breasts, they stroked my nipples with their tips.

Avar slid his hand up my leg. His thumb pressed between my thighs under my skirt, making me whimper from a flash of need.

"I want you, Avar. God, I want you so much…"

"I knew it never was just the collar," he growled with approval, shoving aside my panties and dipping a finger inside me. "Sweetheart, you're delightfully wet all on your own."

I arched my back, taking his finger deeper.

"There is your fault in it too."

"How so?" he rumbled before dragging his tongue over my nipple.

I moaned, pushing my chest into his mouth.

"Why are you so kind to me? So attentive? So…" I jerked my hips as he stroked my clit, making the heat of arousal spike to a new height. "Why are you so good to me, Avar? How am I supposed not to fall for you?"

He lifted his face to mine and echoed my question with his own, "How am I supposed to give you up?"

I trembled, my knees giving in. He caught me, holding me gently in his arms and the loops of his tentacles.

Getting up, he placed me on the table.

"Tonight, you're mine," he said. "Fully and completely."

I opened my legs for him in response.

A pink glow rushed through him in a bright flash. He groaned, leaning over me to kiss my lips, then my chest. Propping his hands on each side of me, he cradled me in the coils of his tentacles.

"All of you is mine tonight," he said firmly, thrusting his hips forward between my thighs.

Heat coursed through my body as he entered me. Slowly, as if holding back, he slid deeper until I took him all.

How he fit, I didn't know, but I enjoyed all of it, every thick inch of his cock.

He paused, hovering over me on outstretched arms, then growled like a wild beast, thrusting harder. The tip of his tentacle found my hot, throbbing clit. My toes curled; my mouth fell open as pleasure rushed me.

He took, and there was nothing I could do to resist it. I gave, unable to stop.

Gripping his forearms, I held on to him in the whirlwind of passion. Mind-blinding pleasure exploded through my body like fireworks. I dug my fingernails into his arms, riding the bliss, wave after wave.

"Maddy, I can't," he groaned. "I can't hold it back any longer."

"Stay." I tried to hold on to his arms, wishing for us to stay connected for as long as we could before we had to part for good.

But he leaned back, sliding out of me.

His glow undulated through his large frame in waves of pink and purple so dark, it almost seemed black.

With my hands propped behind me, I rose to look at him. His erection jolted between his thick, muscular thighs. Smaller than my forearm at first, his hard length suddenly grew to a size bigger than my thigh as I stared, stunned.

Ripples of bright violet and magenta spread from his groin through his entire body. He tossed his head back with a mighty roar that shook the mountain. His giant frame shuddered, sending him forward. Wrapping me in his arms, he propped his elbows on the table.

Waves of every shade of purple from lavender to mauve to eggplant rolled through Avar as he panted, catching his breath.

I took his face between my hands, watching the kaleido-scope of colors changing in his eyes as well.

"It's stunning..." I whispered in awe. "Yours is the most beautiful orgasm I've ever seen."

He smiled with a squint at me. "I wish you could see yours from my vantage point."

"How can mine even compare? I don't sparkle or glow when I come. Or grow a dick the size of a human leg."

He grunted, straightening and taking me with him.

"My dear Maddy, you are the most beautiful sight when you moan and tremble while overcome by passion from my touch. I love watching you come undone. In fact, I love it so much, I want to see it again, right now." He flicked my nipple, placing a kiss on my lips.

I pressed my legs together with a new spasm of desire in my core.

"Where are we going?" I asked as he walked out of the room and down the path around the mountain.

"To my bedroom, where I can fuck you properly and watch you come again."

"But I was supposed to go to Nerifir tonight."

"You're not going anywhere until you've been thoroughly satisfied and then well rested. We'll leave tomorrow."

"*We?* Didn't you say there was no point in you coming since you'd be only an apparition in that world?"

"An apparition is better than nothing. I'm not letting you go alone."

Come to think of it, Avar's mere appearance was a great protection already. Anyone, even a werewolf, would surely run away whimpering like a puppy at the sight of Avar's glowing giant self. With him, it'd be safer than without.

Madison

"Well, I think I'm ready." I adjusted the wide belt around my waist.

The belt had several sewn-on pockets and attached pouches that Avar had filled with all the things he thought might come in handy in Nerifir. I had gold and precious gemstones to trade with, a tin of healing salve, and a brutal looking knife for "just in case." Apparently, werewolves weren't that easily killed. A gun wouldn't do much to stop them. A blade made from Nerifir iron was far more effective. I just hoped it would not come down to me needing to use it on this trip.

"I put a sandwich in one of the pockets too. In case you get hungry," Avar fussed with getting me ready. "The water bag goes here." He attached a filled leather bag to my belt. "Oh, and take this one as well." He handed me something that looked like a length of black cord with purple markings.

"A snake?" I shrank back, realizing what it actually was.

"This is a horned harpy viper," Avar explained. "A highly poisonous kind. This one is long dead, of course, stuffed with sawdust and no longer dangerous. But I read that werewolves are so terrified of harpy vipers, they run away at the mere sight of it, dead or alive."

"All right." I gingerly accepted the snake and rolled it into a coil, carefully trying to avoid the three pairs of sharp horns on its head. "I'm kind of looking forward to running into some werewolves now." I smiled, stuffing the snake into a pouch on my belt. "It'll be a shame if I don't get to see at least one after all this preparation."

"Werewolves resemble humans most of the time. They turn to beasts only on the full moon. But if it's a full moon or close to it when we arrive, we're turning around and going straight back through the portal, Maddy. Do you understand?"

"Without the horologe, though, we won't return to our time."

He shook his head adamantly.

"I'm not risking you running into a beast. If there's a full moon, please promise me you'll turn around and leave without even going ashore. Otherwise, I won't let you go at all. Our deal is off."

At this point, I would be severely disappointed if he called off the whole thing. The plan was clear and seemed easy enough to execute. After getting to the Sarnala Kingdom in Nerifir, I'd go straight to the monastery and convince the nuns to give or sell the horologe to me. I even had a great story prepared about the horologe being the lost family heirloom that held sentimental value to me. According to Avar, the nuns didn't know the true value of the device, which probably made one of them the perfect "trusted keeper" that Evior mentioned in his book.

"If it's a full moon, we can try again later, at some other

time," Avar insisted. "Once we get the horologe eventually, we can return to this time then. I can't have you hurt, Maddy."

Well, I didn't want to get hurt either.

"Fine," I agreed. "If the moon is full, I'll turn around and leave. There will always be another chance, right?"

"Probably."

Using his massive bundle of keys, he opened one of the glass cabinets along the path around his mountain and got out a silver tray with a crystal carafe filled with burgundy liquid.

"A glass of wine before hitting the road?" I quipped.

He smirked, pouring an equal amount of liquid in two crystal glasses that matched the carafe.

"It's the transcendence potion, Maddy. We both need to drink it to travel to your world from here."

"Should I bring it with me? For you to come back here after you drop me off?" If I succeeded at getting the horologe, Avar would be returning to Purgatory alone, without me. My heart squeezed with an ache at the thought of parting from him, but it had to be done.

"No. I don't need the potion to return home." He held up both glasses, not offering me one yet. "Are you sure this is what you want, Maddy?" he asked softly.

I didn't reply right away, considering his question very carefully. After only a short time in Purgatory, I already had a lot to lose by leaving here. My throat tightened as I took a long look around me, quietly saying goodbye to this place. It was hard. But I wasn't done with the living to spend the rest of my life among the dead.

I nodded, not trusting my voice to speak. At last, he offered me one of the glasses, not saying a word either. We drank the potion in silence. It tasted fruity and pleasantly sweet.

Avar took my empty glass from me and set it down next to his. His tentacles circled me in the familiar embrace. He had to hold me so we wouldn't be separated upon arrival to the human world.

"It's a good thing you keep the potion under a lock," I said. "It tastes so good, I would've drunk it long ago, without knowing what it does."

"You're not alone." He shook his head. "Some of my brothers can't be trusted with it, either."

His last words reached me like an echo of a dream. The glass-covered space on the side of the mountain spun out of focus. The sunny sky blended with Avar's purple glow, both washed away by a bright white light that forced me to close my eyes.

I exhaled the warm, lilac-rich air of Purgatory and inhaled much cooler air that was saturated with far less pleasant scents. The smell of gasoline fumes and wet concrete was subtle. But it seemed pungent to me, unused to breathing it lately.

It smelled like home. Thoughts and worries from my past rushed me. My mom must've been devastated after getting my letter with half-baked explanations about my moving away, heartfelt goodbyes, and instructions to sell the restaurant. That was so out of character for me, I wondered if Mom had called the police and reported me as a missing person. Avar had no idea what mess he had started by taking me.

But now, I had a chance to fix it all.

I opened my eyes. We stood on a riverbank with a highway running along it in the distance. It was evening, just before sunset. Other than the muffled sound of traffic, the place seemed deserted, which was a good thing, since the massive, glowing entity from another world held me in his arms, standing in the open.

There was a slight change in Avar's appearance. He no longer looked as tangible as he did back in Purgatory. The outline of his shape blurred. And there was far more give under my hand when I pushed into him. He felt like a dense cloud of light and warmth. And he looked very much like the apparition he'd warned me he'd be in Nerifir.

Only unlike in Nerifir, on Earth, he could still handle things. The sensation of his arms holding me was gentle but real.

"The portal is that way." He turned toward the river.

As we approached, I noticed a faint pink shimmer in one spot over the water. It looked like a reflection of the starting sunset or...a gateway to another world.

"We'll have to dive," Avar explained.

He'd said the portal wouldn't be open for long. Apparently, the portals existed in many places on Earth where the River of Mists connected with our world. But they rarely remained open throughout the day, appearing and disappearing regularly.

"Once we're in the water, you'll have to hold on to me for as long as you can, and I'll hold on to you," he instructed. "We can't get separated, Maddy. If we do, we may end up in different time periods or even in different worlds."

I nodded. He'd gone through all of that with me back in Purgatory already, but I didn't mind the recap. It was hard to grasp it all at once because of how different this experience was compared to anything I'd done before.

I didn't know exactly what part of the human world we were in, but this was not swimming weather. The breeze seeped through my thin clothes. But since I had to go into the water to cross to Nerifir, it made sense not to wear many heavy layers that could drag me under. I had a long skirt on, but only because it fit better with the fashion of Nerifir and would help me blend in and attract less attention if anyone spotted me.

"Now, hold on and listen to my voice," Avar said, wading into the river.

The water licked my feet, instantly filling my boots and drenching my socks. I shivered. It proved even colder than I'd anticipated.

"Maddy, say the word, and I'll turn back," Avar offered.

Back to Purgatory. Back to being stuck between two worlds, not truly belonging to one and unable to return to the other.

"No." I flexed my arms around him. "Let's keep going."

"Hold your breath," he told me as we approached the pink shimmering cloud of mist.

I did as he said. We dove. I clenched my jaw, my body going rigid in the cold water. But the sensation didn't last long. Warmth emitted from Avar, and I pressed myself into him.

"You can breathe now," Avar said suddenly.

I drew in a lungful of air but kept my eyes closed. The darkness of the water was replaced by shimmering light dancing outside of my closed eyelids.

"Now hold your breath again, sweetheart," Avar instructed softly. "Almost there. Once you feel the water again, let go of me and swim."

I nodded, keeping both my eyes and mouth closed.

The water felt warmer this time. I forgot about needing to let go of Avar, holding on to him for dear life. But suddenly, my arms felt empty. I flexed them tighter, hugging nothing but water.

Avar was gone.

Panic urged me to move my arms. My lungs strained, begging for another breath. I kicked my feet, hoping I was swimming up to the surface instead of in any other direction.

The water broke over my head. It sluiced down my face and splashed with waves. I trod it, spitting the water out of my mouth and nose. It tasted briny with salt—not a river anymore but a sea or an ocean.

"Swim toward the light, Maddy," Avar's voice sounded nearby, easing my fear. He was here after all.

I opened my eyes, searching for the light he'd mentioned.

It was dark, it must be night. The only light came from the faint pink shimmer of the portal a short distance away, from the stars above, and from the crescent of the moon in the sky. It wasn't a full moon. We did good.

The light.

What light did he mean?

Kicking the water, I turned around, finally spotting a faint yellow dot of light in the long dark blot of the shore. It didn't appear to be too far, which was a relief, since I wasn't the strongest swimmer.

The surf pushed me closer. And after just a couple of strokes, I felt the sandy bottom under my feet, then waded out of the water, glad to be on solid ground once again.

"Well, so far, so good." I wiped the water out of my face, catching my breath. "It's not a full moon. The monastery is right up the hill, isn't it? The light must be the lantern on its bell tower, like Evior wrote. The only difficulty I can foresee right now is that the nuns are asleep, and I'll have to wait until morning to speak to someone."

It was warmer here than back in my world, which was also a plus since my clothes were soaking wet now.

"Avar?" I turned around to look for him since I'd heard no response.

He wasn't there. No glow, no shape of an apparition, not even a hint of a ghost, only the dark forest edging the beach, the stars above, and the waves of the sea lazily rolling ashore.

I was alone in this dark, strange world.

Panic speared through me.

"Avar!"

Avar

"Avar! Where are you?" Maddy's voice rang with panic, sending a spear of alarm through me too.

"I'm here." I stepped closer to her. "I didn't go anywhere."

"Oh, thank God." She pressed a hand to her chest, releasing a long breath. "I thought I lost you." She turned around again. "But where *here?* I can't see you..."

I stretched both arms and tentacles in front of me, but I couldn't see either of them. There was only the sand of the beach in front and under me.

"Fuck."

"What is it?" Maddy's voice shook. "What's happening to you? Are you okay? Are you really here?"

I was there. Sadly, the only proof of that to her seemed to be my voice.

"I'm completely invisible," I said. "There isn't even an apparition of me, is there?"

She shook her head. "Not that I can see."

As a human who came from the world that believed in my existence, Maddy would sense my presence better than anyone else in Nerifir. If she couldn't see me, no one else would.

"We're going back." I turned around toward the portal, wading through the water that didn't even stir around my legs.

In this world, I was less than air. When air moved, it made waves. Yet I couldn't stir even a single drop.

"Do we have to?" she asked from behind me.

I stopped, realizing that she didn't move from the beach.

"Maddy, sweetheart, let's leave, now," I coaxed gently.

She rotated between me and the light from the monastery that obviously tempted her to enter the forest.

"We're here already. The place is right there." She gestured at the light. "It'd be a waste to just turn around and leave."

The horologe was almost literally in arm's reach. Tingles of anticipation ran through me in a swell. Few things were more exciting than that moment of taking possession of something no one else could ever have.

Except that I was about to lose someone who had become far more precious to me than anything I'd ever owned. I was prepared to lose her by honoring our deal and giving her what she wanted. But I refused to put her in harm's way, even for the sake of her own happiness.

"It's not worth it, Maddy. What if someone attacks you? I can't even scare them away if they can't see me."

"Who is going to attack me?" She spread her arms wide, pausing to let me listen to the stillness of the night. "There's no one here. I have a knife in case of an animal attack. And if a nun happens to be mean to me, you can roar at her. Visible or not, you have enough growl in you to terrify an army."

Displeasure rumbled in my throat, and Maddy giggled.

"See? That snarl right there is enough to send anyone running for the hills."

The stubborn woman wouldn't move from her spot, dead set to get what she came here for. In this world, I didn't even have arms or tentacles to grab her and drag her to safety.

"I'll be careful," she promised sweetly, and I found it impossible to deny anything to that smile of hers. "At the first sign of danger, you'll start yelling and roaring, and I'll run back here to the portal right away."

Unlike many portals between the worlds of the River of Mists, this one never closed. The way back to safety would remain open for her. I scanned the dark woods that surrounded the beach on the border between Sarnala, the kingdom of were-wolves, and Olathana Ocean, where the sirens reigned. I listened carefully. The surf in the bay wasn't too strong, but its measured swishing against the sandy beach drowned out any other sound.

I read that werewolves had driven all the dangerous preda-tors out of these woods. No animal could stand against the packs of blood-hungry werewolves afflicted by Moon Madness during the night of the full moon.

On a night like this, when the moon was still growing, there was little danger in this remote area from either animals or people.

"All right," I gave in, joining Maddy on the beach. "We'll proceed until the first sign of danger."

"Deal." She beamed, and I would've given every priceless thing from my collection for the ability to kiss her right now.

She entered the woods, and I stayed close, scanning our surroundings. The surf stayed behind us, and the usual sounds of the night forest filled the air. Rustling of leaves in the breeze. Small animals scurrying in the underbrush. The occasional hoot of an owl in the distance.

"It doesn't look that much different from our human world, does it?" Maddy mused. "If one doesn't look too closely, that is. The difference is in details. Like those puffy yellow mushrooms, for example." She stepped around the ring of *kibia* mushrooms with their yellow cups spotted with bright orange dots.

"Don't touch them," I warned. If eaten, the mushrooms had a devastating effect on werewolves' shifting cycles. It remained unknown whether they carried any harm to humans, but I wasn't going to risk Maddy's life to find out.

"I'm not touching them," she said quickly. "I'm not here to explore, just to get the horologe and go back home."

"Good girl," I approved.

I wanted to give her what she wished for the most—her freedom. But not at the price of her health or her life.

For the first time in my existence, the desire to give overpowered the urge to possess. The realization struck me into a stupor. I stopped, unable to move my invisible limbs.

For me, the prize in our deal had never been the horologe, though I had to have it now in order to close our bargain and give Maddy her freedom. But the true reason I made that deal was Maddy's tears. I realized I'd do anything in my power to never see her cry again.

Her happiness had become the biggest treasure for me, bigger than even the pleasure of having her in my possession.

She moved ahead meanwhile, muttering something about the glowing moss that grew on the trunks of the trees in the forest.

A crunch of a twig under someone's paw or...a *foot* jolted me with alarm.

"Maddy." I rushed after her. "Listen—"

Two men slipped into her path, like shadows emerging from the forest.

She froze, startled.

I didn't care who they were or even what intentions they had. They were strangers, and that was enough for my worry to spike.

"Back off!" I yelled. "Maddy. Run!"

She spun on her heel. One of the men grabbed her from behind. She squeaked, crushed in his grip.

"Let her go!" I roared, crashing into him.

The burning need to annihilate the bastard raged through me. I grabbed for him to tear him to pieces. But my hands came back empty. My punches met no resistance. And my threats had no effect.

"Let me go!" Maddy screamed, kicking her feet, as one of the assholes held her from behind.

A kick landed on his shin. He cursed, releasing her from his hold. The moment she tried to run, however, he drew his sword and aimed it at her neck.

"Where are you going?" he demanded.

"Who are you?" The other one stepped behind her, blocking her way back to the beach.

"Don't you dare touch her, you fucking pricks!" I raged. "You cursed blobs of slime! If so much as a hair falls off her head, *your* heads will roll. I'll feed you to the sirens and their pet sharks."

"Are you a spy for the rebels?" one of the thugs asked Maddy calmly, as if I hadn't spoken at all.

"Did you not hear what I said?" I roared. "Leave her alone!"

The pale moonlight colored Maddy's brown skin with silver, making her look almost like an apparition herself.

"I don't think they can hear you..." she said, her voice breaking off, her eyes opening wide in horror. "Only I can."

13

Madison

As useless as Avar's threats were at scaring anyone, for me at least, they proved comforting to hear. Judging by their hostile expression, the men accosting me in the dark woods promised trouble. And if so, I loved imagining them being fed to the sirens' pet sharks.

The one with the sword poked its sharp end against my throat.

"Start speaking. Now. Are you a spy?" he asked in a language I had never heard before but now understood perfectly. "Or I'll err on the safe side and kill you right here and now."

Avar roared another explosion of threats peppered with filthy curses, but his words were laced with desperation that stemmed from helplessness. He couldn't stop these two from doing whatever they wanted to me. My life was fully in my hands now.

"I..." I cleared my throat, willing my voice not to shake. "I'm not a spy." Incredibly, the words came out in the same language that the men spoke. It cost me no effort to switch, coming more naturally than speaking my mother tongue.

Neither of the men looked convinced by my answer. The one with the sword at my neck squinted at me suspiciously. His medium blond hair looked like it glowed blue in the spots where the moonlight hit it through the tree branches above.

"Where are you going?" he demanded, then brushed his hand down his shirt that was now damp from my clothes since he'd grabbed me. "And why are you wet?"

My mind reeling, I scrambled for an answer that wouldn't possibly make the situation even worse for me. Panic seemed to paralyze my brain, however, and I couldn't come up with anything.

"I'm...I..."

Would it make sense to tell the truth? Would they believe me?

"Tell them you're from a fishing boat that capsized out in the ocean," Avar's tense voice reached me, stretching like a lifeline across the sea of panic. "You made it ashore but got separated from the others."

"I'm from a fishing boat..." I repeated mechanically.

What if they asked for more details?

I knew dozens of ways to cook all possible kinds of fish, but very little about how to catch any.

"What fishing boat?" The blond man demanded.

"It capsized out there, in the ocean." I waved back toward the beach. "I don't know where the others are. We got separated in the water."

The second man walked closer from behind me.

"She's lying, Ider," he spat through his teeth. "There are more rebel spies in the High Lord's lands than there are fleas on a mutt."

"I'm not a spy," I insisted.

What rebels were they talking about, anyway? What High Lord?

"Who were the others on the boat with you?" Ider kept interrogating me.

"Who?" I echoed, my mind going blank again. "Um…"

"Your father and two brothers," Avar helpfully supplied. "You come from Lenora fishing village, on the southern end of the border with Olathana."

"Why were you sailing here?" Ider's voice came clipped from impatience.

"I'm from Lenora fishing village. It's south… I mean, on the southern end of the border with Olathana. I was fishing with my dad and brothers."

"It's a long way from Lenora to here," the other man drawled, his stare scanning my face and clothes carefully.

"It has to be a village far away from here," Avar explained. "Otherwise, they would expect to have seen you before."

"Right," I agreed, then explained to the men, "It was a long trip, but the fishing was good, so we kept going. We had just decided to go back when the boat turned over in the dark. I saw the light out there," I pointed in the direction of the monastery, "and thought I could get help to look for my family. I hope they're all right," I added with a sob, trying to act like a woman in distress who might've just lost her family to the treacherous waters. "They aren't the best swimmers."

"Why *would* they be?" Ider frowned.

His partner shuddered in a gesture similar to a dog shaking water out of its fur.

"Werewolves hate water," Avar said. "They don't swim. But they also don't drown. Water won't kill them."

"Oh." I bit my lip.

It was best not to make up stuff anymore or I risked digging the hole I'd fallen in even deeper.

I pressed both hands to my chest in a plea.

"Please, let me go. I promise I'm not a spy or anything like that. I'll spend the night in the monastery, then look for my family first thing tomorrow morning. I promise we'll never come here again. We'll find some other place to fish."

"How do you know that's a monastery over there?" Suspicion thickened in Ider's voice.

Shit.

As someone from a remote village, I shouldn't have known that, should I?

"I...I've passed by here before. By boat. While fishing." I wished I was better at lying. It was so not my thing.

Ider kept his stare on me. "Let's take her to the High Lord, Zep."

Zep smirked, adjusting his tunic.

"The High Lord likes them much younger than this." He took my chin in his hand. I jerked my head, trying to get away, but Ider pressed his sword into my throat harder. "You're way past your thirties, aren't you?" Zep turned my face up to the moonlight. "No real signs of aging yet. But some of those wrinkles may mean you're getting close. You're like what? Three? Four hundred years old?"

"Hey!" I freed my chin from him, ignoring the sword. "I'm only thirty-two."

"Careful, Maddy," Avar sounded worried as the tip of the sword scraped my skin. "Werewolves live to be five hundred years old at least. They stop aging at around your age, then resume it in the last decade of their lives."

"Way too old for the High Lord," Zep concluded, his smirk spreading like a greasy stain. "Personally, I take them any age, though."

He moved closer and slid his palms up my arms, undeterred by my wet clothes. Dread chilled me.

Avar lost it again.

"Keep your filthy paws off her, you pathetic mutt!" he roared.

"You're not going to fuck a traitor, are you?" Ider snapped with disgust.

"She isn't a traitor. Are you, sweet thing?" Zep murmured, sniffing at my neck.

I recoiled from him as far as his grip on my arms allowed. Thoughts rushed through my brain at a feverish speed.

Do I pretend to be a spy to thwart off his advances and risk being killed? Or do I keep denying it and risk being raped?

The choice was crushing.

A long, blood-curdling howl came from a distance, and all three of us stilled.

"There is that thing again," Zep muttered uncertainly, loosening his grip on me.

"Maddy," Avar said with a strain in his voice. "You have to go back to the portal."

At this point, I was beginning to think that was a good idea too.

"What's howling out there?" I squeezed through my throat that suddenly felt almost too tight to speak.

"I'm not sure." Zep let go of me completely, nervously peering into the darkness around us.

"We have to return to the camp." Ider took a slow turn around. No longer pointing his sword at me, he held it out in front of him. The unknown danger obviously was far greater than anything I could do to them.

Zep drew his sword too.

"You're coming with us." He grabbed my arm, tugging me along.

"Fucking bastard," Avar cursed, running out of breath.

I understood his frustration. However, that terrifying howl came from the direction of the beach. What if I ran into whatever made that noise on my way to the portal?

"I don't think I should go back to the beach," I said to Avar.

Zep gave me a side eye. "No one wants you to go to the beach. We're going back to our camp, then to the High Lord's castle. Just stay close to me or the monster will get you."

"What is that monster? A werewolf?"

Ider snorted a laugh. "Are we monsters now? Since when?"

In the land of werewolves, I should've known better than to call them monsters. Especially since they believed I was one of them.

"No one knows what that thing is, all right?" Zep nervously scratched his arm through the long sleeve of his tunic. "It's been howling and roaring all night out there, louder than a normal werewolf would even on the night of a full moon. I'd say we get back to the camp, grab Krim, and head out to the castle right away."

"Didn't we decide to camp in the woods until morning?" Ider walked a step ahead of us, watching the path carefully, with his sword ready.

"Fuck these woods." Zep spat on the ground. "I don't want to stay here another hour if I don't have to."

The forest gave me an eerie feeling, too, now. All its colors and glow turned from pretty and whimsical to creepy and menacing.

The howling came again. This time it was interspersed with rumbling roars, as if the beast was tearing apart something or *someone*.

Our small group went as still as statues.

"Maddy," Avar spoke first. "I need to see what the hell that is."

"Don't leave me!" I begged. What if he couldn't find me once he'd left? Even if he was just a disembodied voice, I needed him close. "Let's just stay together, okay?"

Ider squinted at me. "Who are you talking to?"

"No one," I said quickly, then thought of something else to try. "Actually, I'm talking to my pet snake." I reached into a pouch on my belt. "Here, want to see?" I uncoiled the horned harpy viper, thrusting it toward him.

Zep flinched, as did Ider. Their expressions, however, were more cautious than terrified. Not exactly the reaction I'd hoped for.

Zep sniffed the air. "It's dead."

Ider curled his lips in disgust. "Why are you carrying a dead viper with you?"

My shoulders slumped in disappointment. Neither of the werewolves ran for the hills in horror like Avar had said they would.

"That just proves it, doesn't it? One can't trust everything one reads." I coiled the snake back together again, wondering if I could somehow benefit from them thinking I was crazy. "Come here, baby," I cooed, tucking the snake back into the pouch. "You don't have to hang out with these guys. They don't appreciate you, anyway."

Zep arched an eyebrow, staring at me. Ider just shook his head, turning his attention back to the forest ahead of us and the danger that might be lurking in there.

"It's a *dead* snake, woman," Zep insisted, looking dumbfounded.

"Shh." I brought a finger to my lips. "She's sleeping. Let her rest. She's had a horrible day with the boat capsizing and stuff."

"Maddy, are you all right?" Avar asked carefully, with worry lacing his voice.

"I'm fine, sweetie." I patted the pouch gently. "No need to worry. We'll find a way to safety. I promise."

Zep scoffed, turning to Ider. "Either the salt water messed up her brain today or she's always been a bit…" he moved his finger over his temple in a circular motion, "…*off*, up there."

Ider shrugged. "Maybe one good reason to keep her around is so that we can throw her at the beast if it ever comes too close. Let him eat her while we run away."

The familiar rumble sounded just above my ear.

"I'll feed them to wild beasts myself," Avar growled. "I'll find a way. I swear."

"Just ignore them, sweetie." I petted the pouch with the dead snake soothingly. "They're not worth your time."

Both Zep and Ider paid little attention to my talking now, which allowed me some communication with Avar in their presence.

The further we walked, the more distance we put between us and the beach. With the mysterious creature prowling in these woods, running back to the portal no longer felt much safer than sticking with Zep and Ider for now. At least, they were too scared for their own hides to even think about hurting me at the moment.

We circled the monastery, putting it between us and the beach. Some distance after that, the dancing light of a campfire came into view from between the tree trunks, and my guards visibly relaxed.

As we came closer, a dark-haired man stepped from behind the trees to greet us. Dressed in the similar way to Zep and Ider in a linen tunic and a pair of long pants tucked into short boots, he held a knife in one hand and a sword in the other.

"Hi Krim." Sheathing his sword, Ider went straight for the blankets spread by the fire and started packing them up.

"Change of plans. We're heading out of the woods tonight. There is no need to wait for the morning."

"Did you hear all that noise?" Krim's eyes roamed over the trees behind us. "What the fuck was that?"

"The howling, you mean?" Zep plucked a sole piece of charred meat from a skewer by the fire and took a bite.

"Yes, the howling. It came so close at one point, I thought the creature might get me. I thought it got both of you already." His wild gaze finally landed on me. "Who's she?"

With his knee on a blanket roll while he tightened a leather belt around it, Ider glanced my way. "We're not sure who she is. Might be a fisherman's daughter, or a rebel spy, or both. We're taking her to the castle for the High Lord to decide what to do with her."

Krim slid a quick glance up and down my figure. "You *know* what he'll do with her."

Zep shook his head. "No, he won't like her. She's too old, over thirty already."

"I meant he'd do what he always does with the rebels. He'd keep her in a cage until the next full moon, then tie her to a tree in the forest overnight."

Dread trickled down my spine with cold sweat. Being tied up during a full moon when every werewolf in the area would be roaming the woods, looking for blood, meant certain death. A gruesome, painful death.

I shivered in horror.

"We won't let it get that far, Maddy," Avar assured me. "You're not going to the castle with them."

I wished to believe him with all my heart, even as I had no idea how to get away from them.

"Well..." Ider gathered some pots and cups from around the campfire, emptied them, then tied them to his blanket roll.

"That's the least those filthy rebels deserve for opposing the High Lord and refusing to worship the Moon Goddess Ghata."

"Ghata," I repeated the name softly.

"These men must be the scouts of High Lord Fromir," Avar explained. "After the werewolves rebelled against Ghata's brutalities, the High Lord supported her."

"Who will win in the end?" I asked. "The High Lord or the rebels?"

I turned to my pouch with the snake when speaking, but the three men were too busy packing up the camp to listen to me, especially now that they thought I was "not all up there."

"The rebels will win. Eventually," Avar replied.

"Good." I played no part in this conflict, but it made me feel better to know that the cruel and possibly perverted High Lord would be defeated sooner or later.

Zep had finally helped Ider pack, and they were almost done now.

"Tell them you need to use a bathroom," Avar said unexpectedly.

"But I don't need to go."

"Tell them you do," he insisted.

"Almost done, fisher girl." Zep strolled my way. "We'll be in the High Lord's castle by morning. No monsters can get behind those stone walls. You'll be safe."

I highly doubted that. Judging by what they'd said so far, there were plenty of monsters in the High Lord's castle, including the High Lord himself.

"I need to use a bathroom," I said.

Zep laughed. "There're no bathrooms in the forest, silly girl."

"You know what I mean. I need to pee. Or do you want me to pee in my pants?" I shrugged. "Makes no difference to me. My clothes are wet already."

He scrunched his nose in disgust. "But what if the beast gets you?"

"I'll come with you," Avar said.

"You're not watching me pee," I snapped at him.

"That's not what I said." Zep looked confused, but only for a moment. "But if you're offering..."

"God, no." I cringed. "I'd rather take my chances with the monster."

I headed away from the clearing and behind the trees, with Zep thankfully staying behind.

"Now what?" I asked Avar, after putting some distance between me and the camp.

"Don't go too far!" Zep yelled.

"Zep, we're leaving," Ider said with a tight, nervous note in his voice.

"Now, you run, Maddy," Avar urged. "Run all the way to the beach, then to the portal, sweetheart. Don't let them take you to the castle and put you in a cage."

I peered into the dark forest surrounding me. It was a long way back to the portal, with unknown danger lurking out there somewhere. On the other hand, if they locked me in that cage, it'd be only a matter of time until a whole pack of monsters would eat me.

I knew my best chance was to run, but I wondered if I should do it later, after we're out of the woods or maybe closer to the sunrise, when the mysterious beast would hopefully climb back into its lair to sleep. Even the most terrifying monsters had to sleep sometimes, didn't they?

"Hey!" Zep yelled. "Whatever your name is, we're leaving—"

An air-splitting scream cut his words short.

I spun around, and so did Zep.

Backlit by the crackling glow from the dying campfire, a

giant creature pounced on top of Ider. A surreal mix of man and beast, with no neck, and hunched shoulders, it tore into Ider with its long sharp teeth.

Patches of black fur stuck out of the monster's pale skin that appeared to glow in the moonlight. Spiky ears lay flat against its head as it raised its head, blood dripping from its snout.

"Run, Maddy!" Avar roared. The horror in his voice pushed my body into action even as my mind was still frozen in terror.

I sprinted away, as if the monster was already chasing me.

Zep cursed behind me. A sword swished through the air. The beast howled. It was so close, the hair on the back of my neck moved as if the creature was breathing on it already.

I ran, blinded by panic, sliding on dead leaves that covered the ground and tripping over the tree roots. There was nothing ahead of me but darkness. Until I saw the warm, yellow light. I ran toward it without thinking. I had no choice.

"Monastery," Avar's voice came like a beacon in the storm. "Go for it, Maddy."

He sounded out of breath as if he was running too. Most likely, he was catching up with me after trying to fight the monster. I didn't need to ask to know that it didn't work. He'd already tried to fight Zep and Ider. Punches were useless when one had no fists. But even just his voice was better than nothing. I wasn't alone.

"Monastery," I punted, holding the course toward the light.

A building had walls.

"No monsters can get behind those stone walls." Zep's words echoed in my head.

Reaching the monastery before the beast was my only hope.

I climbed up the hill toward the wooden gate in the solid rock wall.

"Please be open," I begged silently, pushing against the gate.

It screeched, opening at an odd angle. I ran into the small, round courtyard. The building of the monastery was shaped like a semi-circle, or a moon crescent, with a tall bell tower in the middle. A large lantern on the very top of the tower shone with the warm yellow light that had guided me here.

Other than the lantern, there was no other light. Every window in the building was dark.

I headed to the front door.

"Let me check first," Avar stopped me.

I paused hesitantly, looking over my shoulder. My heart pounded hard. Fear pricked my skin with goosebumps. I strained my eyes, peering into the darkness behind the broken gate and listened for every sound, expecting the beast to jump out at any second.

"Get in, Maddy," Avar said just a moment later. "The door is unlocked and there's no one in the front hall."

I didn't wait for him to tell me twice. Slipping inside, I closed the heavy wooden door behind me and leaned against it, finally catching my breath.

With no windows in the hall, I could see nothing but darkness. I felt the uneven wood of the door behind me but found no lock. Moving along the wall, I found a piece of furniture, a cabinet or a dresser, I wasn't sure, but it seemed heavy. I shoved it over to block the door.

Would it be enough to keep that creature away?

I shuddered, remembering its blood-soaked snout and glowing red eyes.

"Maddy." Avar's voice softened as he probably saw how terrified I was. "We left him behind. He was too busy to chase you. I checked."

Too busy eating Ider and probably Zep right after.

"Okay. Thanks." I could only manage the briefest of sentences between my ragged breaths.

"Stay here," Avar instructed. "I'll see what's in the other rooms. If this building is safe, you'll stay here for the rest of the night."

I nodded, sliding down the door to the floor.

My breathing scratched my dry throat. I unhooked the water bag from my belt and took a few gulps. My hands shook so much, the water splashed on my chest.

"Fuck," I cursed softly, corking the water bag and putting it away.

This whole trip turned out to be much scarier than I could've imagined. But I was still alive. That was something.

From one of the pockets on my belt, I got the sandwich that Avar had packed for me back on his nice, safe, and quiet mountain in Purgatory.

I wasn't hungry. At the mere thought of the monster lurking out there in the woods, my stomach roiled with fear and repulsion. But if I had to run again any time soon, I needed some food for energy.

The smell of cheese and roast beef was far more pleasant than the stench of fear clinging to every pore of my body. I took a bite and chewed, wondering what was taking Avar so long. How many rooms did this place have?

A scurrying noise came from the top of the dresser above me. Then, something furry dropped into my lap.

I jumped, a mouthful of sandwich choking my scream.

Sharp claws grabbed onto my skirt with a loud, displeased "Meow!"

"A cat?" I pressed my hand to my chest, trying to calm my heart that had almost leaped out through my throat. "A fucking cat."

The gray tabby cat quickly found the sandwich I'd dropped on the floor in panic, then pulled a slice of roast beef out of it.

"Great." I considered fighting the rascal for the rest of the sandwich, then decided to let him have it. "Do the nuns not feed you here?"

The cat paid me no attention, calmly devouring my roast beef.

A narrow ray of moonlight fell on the floor next to the cat, bringing my attention up to the small window above the door. The shutter had been moved open by the animal as he must've climbed through it to get inside.

"Nice. You have your own entrance up there," I said.

Pet doors usually were cut in the bottom, close to the floor. But maybe the cat liked climbing roofs more than walking on the ground. Or nuns simply didn't want to let snakes and rodents into their monastery, since the cat clearly didn't know how to close the shutter behind him.

The dim light illuminated a large female figurine on the dresser that I hadn't noticed in the darkness before. It was carved from a milky-blue stone that shimmered brightly when the moonlight hit it.

At the feet of the figurine, five phases of the moon were laid out in smaller stones of the same glowing rock. I lifted one of the stones, admiring the pretty sparkles inside it.

The cat jumped onto the dresser, startling me again.

"You've got to stop doing that," I hissed at him, shoving the stone into one of the pockets on my belt. "My nerves are already rattled without you adding to it. What do you want?"

My sandwich lay open on the floor, without even a shred of meat left in it.

"That was fast," I said as the cat rubbed its head on my arm. "If you came for more, I don't have any. Eat the cheese now, you spoiled little brat."

I spotted a thick metal collar around the cat's neck with a round tag on the front.

"What's your name?" I lifted the tag.

Keeper was written inside the ring of aged bronze.

"Keeper?" I stared at the cat's collar. "Is that what they call you?"

Lined with leather, the collar was made with a row of thin, overlaying metal gears. Smaller gears and dials were inlaid between and over them. I could read the numbers and letters engraved on the dials but had no idea what any of them meant when put together like that. Plates of the same glowing rock sparkled inside the gears.

"What is this thing you're wearing, *Keeper?*"

"Evior says he left the horologe in care of a trusted keeper in a women's monastery," Avar's words echoed through my mind.

Could that be that the nuns weren't the ones in charge of the device?

Did the horologe just literally fall into my lap?

Did I find what I'd come here for, after all?

And it only cost me a sandwich.

A long, deafening roar tore from inside the building, reverberating between the walls and making the blood in my veins freeze with horror.

"Run, Maddy!" Avar shouted. "Run! Now."

14

Avar

Unease prickled through me when I left Maddy alone in the dark hall of the monastery, but I needed to know what was in and around the building where she took shelter. I had to make sure it was safe for her to spend the night here.

I saw the beast devouring the two werewolves who'd captured Maddy. In that way, he actually did me a favor by doing my work for me. Those two deserved nothing less for the way they treated Maddy.

If the monster hunted for food, the flesh of the High Lord's scouts should satisfy him. I hoped he went back to his lair by now and was already falling asleep with his belly full.

Maddy was safe on her own for the few minutes that it'd take me to make sure nothing dangerous was lurking in the building. The advantage of having no physical presence in this world was that I could move freely through walls. Closed doors didn't stop me.

I swiftly went through the monastery's large gathering hall, then the dining hall. There were praying rooms, each with a shrine to the Moon Goddess Ghata with a figurine or a picture of her.

All the rooms were empty. The nuns might've gone down into the cellar to hide after hearing the howls in the woods. They had cages underground where they stayed during the full moon. According to a scroll I read, this order practiced peace and refrained from murder and violence, even in their werewolf form.

Next were the nuns' private rooms.

I slipped through a closed door and nearly gagged. Despite the broken window, the air in the narrow dorm was saturated with the warm, heavy stench of blood.

A woman lay on the floor by the bed, her eyes frozen open in horror. Her chest was torn from her chin to her waist, her nightshirt soaked in blood, her throat ripped out.

A growl came from outside the window.

The monster jumped onto the windowsill, his bulk obscuring the moonlight. His red eyes roamed the space as if searching for something, but they didn't stop on me. Just like everyone else in this world, he couldn't see me.

I saw him perfectly well, however.

It was no man and no beast, but an ugly, grotesque mix of both. Backlit by the moonlight, he gripped the window frame with his right hand. His pale skin glowed in places where it wasn't covered by black fur. Black lines of a tattoo stood out, covering his entire right arm.

"You're one of Ghata's *bracks*, aren't you?" It dawned on me. "Or you used to be before something forced you to go berserk."

Bracks, the goddess's monks, were marked with a large tattoo around their necks and down their right arms. They mostly looked like humans. However, this one appeared like a creature from a nightmare.

The monster jumped into the room, ignoring the dead nun. Clearly, he didn't hunt for food. He killed for blood, for the sheer brutality of murder and mutilation. With him here, nobody of blood and flesh was safe.

"Maddy!" I rushed back through all the rooms as the monster howled behind me.

She stood by the dresser, alarm etched on her face.

"Run!" I shouted.

She grabbed an animal from the dresser.

"Is that a racoon?" I yelled, dumbfounded.

What was she doing?

"It's a cat." She went to move the dresser while holding the cat under her arm.

"Leave it. You have no time. You need to get out of here. Use the window in the room to the right."

Thank goodness, she listened, leaving the dresser but not letting go of the damn cat. Pressing it to her chest, she ran into the front room. The window here was broken too. A dead nun lay under it in a puddle of blood, her throat slashed with ragged wounds. Another one was by the door, her head ripped off her shoulders.

The berserker had been here before, spreading violence and death. He came back just for Maddy, and he wouldn't stop hunting her until she was dead too.

She gasped, frozen in horror at the sight of the dead bodies.

"Out the window, Maddy," I hurried. "Run back to the gate."

Snapping out of her stupor, she climbed out and ran outside.

"Now where?" She turned around just past the gate, looking disoriented.

Sadly, even after losing the visibility and strength of a physical presence, I didn't gain the ability to soar or fly like a spirit. But the building stood on a hill, and I was taller than her. I saw the shimmering line of the ocean in the distance.

"To your left and down the hill. Run!"

She sprinted in the direction I told her, chased by the frustrated roars of the beast searching for her inside.

"*Run, sweetheart, run,*" I begged in my mind. "*And be fast. Your life is in your legs right now.*"

Death was just a transition, a passageway from one world to another. But dying from the monster's teeth would hurt, and I couldn't stand the thought of Maddy getting hurt in any way.

Fear I never knew before racked me. We were in another world, one that had its own afterlife that didn't include Purgatory. If Maddy's soul left her body here, would it remain trapped in this world for eternity?

What if I risked losing her forever?

Horror sliced through me like a knife.

Run, Maddy.

She did. She dashed like a woman possessed down the hill, weaving between the trees and jumping over fallen branches. The moonlight and the glow from the moss gave just enough light for her to find the way.

"Keep to the left," I instructed, noticing that she'd strayed off course a little.

She corrected her direction, not slowing her pace.

The dreadful howl came from the woods behind us. It was much closer than the monastery we'd left behind. The *brack* was on Maddy's trail.

"Keep going," I urged.

She was fast, but I feared not fast enough. The monster was gaining on her. The cat squirmed in her arms, unhappy with being jolted around like that.

"Drop the cat, Maddy."

It would make a good snack for the beast. Maybe the cat would distract the monster enough to buy Maddy a few precious seconds to escape.

"No," she punted, pressing the damn thing tighter to her chest.

"I'm not losing you over a fucking cat. Drop it."

She just glared in my direction, pressing on down the hill.

The beach was close. I could already hear the swishing of the surf from behind the trees.

"Almost there, sweetheart," I urged her.

But the beast was getting closer too. The crushing of the underbrush came from right behind us.

Maddy ran onto the beach, and the *brack* leaped out of the forest after her.

"Don't look back. Run!" I yelled. "To the portal."

The shimmer of the portal beckoned. Safety was just a few steps and a couple of swim strokes away.

I jumped between Maddy and the *brack*, desperately trying to shield her from his sharp claws and poisonous teeth. But he leaped through me as if I were nothing but air.

"Fuck you, *brack!*" I yelled at its deformed face. "You're nothing but a mindless puppet of Ghata. You're less than an animal. Fight me! Look at me!"

See me.

Maddy ran into the surf. Water slowed her down. The monster leaped across the beach, landing at the water's edge. Ghata's *bracks* came from werewolves, and werewolves disliked water, but the monster hesitated only for a moment. His blood-thirst clearly overpowered his fear of water. Just one more leap, and he'd catch my Maddy.

She was up to her shoulders in the ocean now, holding the screaming, clawing cat above the surface. I pressed my invisible self to her back, wrapping my arms and tentacles around her in a cocoon, wishing with every fiber of my being to protect her, to keep her safe, unharmed, and happy.

Her fear, her desperation, her pain tore me apart. I never felt these emotions as acutely as I felt them through her now.

I would give everything, every single thing I owned, my very existence, for her to survive this unscathed.

All my emotions boiled into one, spreading through me in a new, beautiful feeling. Warm and light, it grew, taking over my entire being.

Love.

I'd never felt it this strongly before, but I recognized it, nevertheless.

It grew so big, if I had a heart, it'd break. But I had no heart to contain my love for Maddy only in it. It spread through me, uncontained. It filled me whole, transcending the worlds.

They didn't believe in me in Nerifir, but there was faith in love everywhere. And it gave me substance, at least in light.

A bright purple glow exploded through my shape. The beast howled mid jump, but not in bloodthirst this time. A stunned whimper mixed into his terrifying howl. In the darkness of the night, my light blinded him.

He stumbled, reaching for Maddy with his clawed hand. It went through me with no resistance, but instead of ripping her head off, his claws only tore the tunic on her back, leaving deep, bloody grooves in her flesh.

"Maddy!" I yelled in anguish.

She gasped a breath and went under. Pushing with both feet against the bottom, she propelled herself toward the glowing column of the portal in the ocean.

A pink glow surrounded us. And the River of Mists took us.

We floated in its magical stream of shimmer.

"Breathe, Maddy," I said.

Please, still be breathing.

Her chest expanded as she inhaled. Her hand fell away from the cat's face, and the fucking thing screamed at the top of his lungs, proving he was still alive too.

The cat scrambled out of Maddy's arms, but there was nowhere for him to run. Time hung suspended here. Gravity didn't exist. Kicking and screaming, the cat floated nearby.

"Come here, kitty," Maddy called softly.

If it was up to me, I would've left the furry thing back at the monastery. He'd already proven he had enough brains to survive a monster attack. He'd make it just fine on his own. But Maddy wanted him for some reason. And if she did, I'd give it to her. I'd give her anything.

I reached with my tentacle, grabbed the cat, and dragged him to her.

"There you go," she cooed, cradling the creature in her arms again. "It's all good. See?" She scratched behind the cat's ear to calm him. "Avar." She tilted her head, looking up at my face. "I can see you again."

She smiled, and I couldn't hold back anymore. Grabbing both her and the cat, I kissed her.

The chilly air of reality invaded the peaceful magical pink flow of the River of Mists.

"Hold your breath again, Maddy."

She sucked in a breath, then placed a hand over the cat's face too.

Feeling the hard ground under my feet again, I rose up from the river, back in the human world.

The blood from the deep wounds on Maddy's back mixed with the water sluicing down my arms, and I didn't even bother walking out to the riverbank.

Instead, I went straight home. To Purgatory.

15

Madison

I tried to move and immediately regretted it. My back burned in agony. Wincing from the pain, I opened my eyes to the view of the familiar lavender sheets under my cheek. I was lying in Avar's bed in his bedroom, face down.

My belt was off. The tunic had been cut open on my back. Its frayed, bloodied edges draped on each side of me, staining Avar's luxurious sheets with rusty red.

"You're awake?" His deep voice sounded above me.

"I think so."

I tried to turn my neck to look up at him, but he was too tall for me to see his face from this position without risking twisting my head off.

"Don't move." He sat on the bed next to me. "You're injured. I couldn't protect you."

The sadness in his voice gutted me. I found his tentacle on the bed next to me and squeezed it.

"Avar, baby, but you did protect me." I lifted my hand to

my eyes to see if I still had my body. It looked like I did. "I'm alive, am I not?"

"Barely." He sighed, opening a jar in his hands. "I cleaned your wounds and was hoping to put this on them before you woke up." He showed me the jar with pale gel inside it. "Now, it'll hurt."

"What is it?"

"A healing ointment. It'll numb the pain. But it'll hurt while I'm putting it on. How are you feeling?"

"Fine, I guess, everything considered." The memories of my mad dash through the woods with the monster breathing down my neck made me nauseous.

Avar hesitated with the jar in his hands. "Would you prefer to wait?"

"No." I rolled my head, pressing my face into the pillow. "Go ahead. Put that thing on. It hurts a lot already, anyway."

Holding the jar in his hands, he leaned over me, then used the tip of his tentacle to gently apply the ointment on my mangled back. The delicate touch of his corollas hardly added any more pain to my wounds.

"How does it look?" I asked, almost grateful that I couldn't see my back.

"It'll heal," Avar replied evasively. "This ointment is very good. It'll hardly leave any scars at all. We're lucky it was his claws and not his venomous teeth that got you. A werewolf's bite is not survivable for a human."

"Was that monster a werewolf then? How did he shift without the full moon?"

"I believe it was one of Ghata's monks, a *brack*. Ghata marks them with a specific tattoo on their neck and arm. This one had it. The *bracks* don't follow the werewolves' usual shifting pattern because they don't obey the moon, only Ghata. She takes over their souls and bodies, filling them with rage.

Rage is what changes their appearance, and this one seemed to have so much of it, he's gone berserk."

A shudder ran through my body. The monster's howling still echoed in my ears. The vision of blood-drenched corpses flashed through my mind.

"He killed people, Avar. And he'll kill more if he isn't stopped."

"He will be stopped, sweetheart. I doubt he'll make it alive through the next full moon. He may be mad with rage and drunk on violence, but he isn't a match to a pack of werewolves in their beast form."

"Good. I don't ever want to see that horrible scowl ever again."

"You won't," Avar promised. "We're never going back to Nerifir."

"Sounds good to me." I nodded as he finished applying the ointment and closed the jar. From the tiny glimpse I took at that world, Nerifir seemed beautiful, but way too dangerous for my liking. Evading cruel high lords and running from terrifying monsters wasn't something I wished to do on an everyday basis. I far preferred my safe, even if a little boring, existence as a restaurant owner. "Why are we here, by the way? Shouldn't I be back home?"

Avar tensed.

"Technically, our deal is off since we didn't find the horologe. However—"

"Oh, but it isn't off. I believe I got what you wanted. What time is it now?" I sat up gingerly, favoring my back.

"Just a few hours later than when we left here." Avar looped his tentacles around me to catch me if I collapsed.

"Aha!" I lifted a finger in the air triumphantly. "We wouldn't have arrived in our time without the horologe, would we?"

"Not necessarily. There is always a chance of that happening—"

"Yes, like a one-in-a-gazillion chance, but I don't think that's what happened with us." I looked around. "Where is the cat?"

"The cat?" Avar blinked, glancing around too. "No idea. Maybe he went to the kitchen for some food?"

"More food? How much can that cat eat? He devoured a pile of roast beef just a short while ago." I made a move to get off the bed, but Avar stopped me.

"Stay here. I'll find the fucking cat."

The moment he opened the bedroom door, however, the cat strolled in, holding both his head and his tail up proudly. He jumped on the bed, licking his whiskers.

"I bet my favorite burner on my stove," I said, "that he found the kitchen and already stole something from it."

Avar glared at the creature as the cat lifted his hind leg and started cleaning the two furry balls under his tail without a lick of shame.

"This thing almost cost you your life," Avar grumped.

"But it will also bring me my life back. Look at his collar."

He leaned over the cat, gently moving the animal's hind paw aside to have an unobstructed view of his neck.

"I'll be damned," he gasped.

I beamed.

"Did I guess it right? Look at the tag. His name is Keeper, as in the Trusted Keeper of the Magical Horologe." I paused, doubt crawling into my mind unbidden. "Please tell me the collar is the horologe that you wanted more than anything."

He slid a finger over the gears on the cat's collar.

"It is most definitely the horologe, Maddy. Only it's not what I want more than anything anymore."

"Really?" I huffed a laugh with a shake of my head. "So, it's true for the sins, too, what they say about humans? One can never be satisfied with what they have."

For the Sin of Greed, that must be more true than for anyone else.

He rested his gaze on me. "Oh, I believe I've finally found someone who would satisfy me fully and completely." He brushed the side of my face with the tip of his fingers. "Stay with me, Maddy."

Time seemed to stop as I stared into his eyes. Oh, how tempting it was to just stay lost in them forever. My old life felt so distant already. It wouldn't be too hard to keep it that way.

Except that...

"I have people depending on me, Avar. Responsibilities..."

Reasons that seemed so solid just a short while ago no longer felt that way.

What had changed?

And suddenly, I knew the answer. I fell in love. There wasn't enough room in my chest for the feeling that overflowed me.

I loved him. Despite my best intentions, I fell for a mortal sin. Hard. And now, leaving him felt like wrenching my heart out of my chest while it was still beating. It hurt worse than any wound.

Yet I also knew that the thoughts of my mother living the rest of her life alone with no one to care for her when she no longer could take care of herself would haunt me for the eternity that lay ahead.

If I stayed, I would never be fully happy.

Normally, souls didn't remember the details of the life they left behind when coming to Purgatory. But I did. My life was unfinished, and I could never truly move on if I left it that way.

"Avar..." I shook my head, choking on the words I had to say. "I can't...I..."

He didn't need any words, reading me better than anyone ever had. His expression fell. Hope left him, dimming his glow. He reached to cup my face but stopped himself and patted my knee instead, then got off the bed, heading for the door.

"I'll bring you some clean clothes to change into and something to eat. Do you want tea as well?"

I swallowed a lump in my throat.

"Tea would be nice."

He took in my crestfallen expression.

"Please don't get upset, Maddy. I can't stand to see you sad. I won't ask you again to stay. I understand."

The moment after Avar left, Keeper climbed into my lap. I scratched behind his ear and sniffed, tears burning my eyes.

Avar stopped looking strange to me a long time ago. I no longer thought of him as an ancient being from another world, or a mortal sin, or some incomprehensible entity. To me, he was just a man I fell in love with, someone I believed I could be happy with, a man I wanted with my whole heart and my very soul.

"Do you think he'll wait for me?" I asked the cat. Petting his soft fur helped keep the tears at bay. "What are a few decades for someone who's lived for millennia, right? But will it be selfish of me to ask him to wait?"

If a soul never died, nothing was forever, not even the most heartbreaking goodbye. Maybe Avar could visit me while we were apart? Seeing him at least occasionally would be better than not seeing him at all.

The mountain shook suddenly. Spooked, the cat leaped up to his paws.

"It's okay, Keeper." I stroked his head soothingly. "It just means we have a visitor—"

The mountain shook again and again. And again. It kept

shaking, with one tremor building upon another, growing into an earthquake that seemed endless.

The heavy dresser by the wall moved. Books and decorations slid from it and crashed to the floor. The room lurched sideways. I screamed, grabbing onto the bedpost. Keeper shot off the bed and out of the door.

It was not just *one* visitor. An entire army must be invading Avar's mountain, shattering the peace of this place like glass.

When the trembling subdued a little, I unclenched my fingers from around the bedpost and scrambled off the bed.

"Avar!" I swung the door open.

A giant flaming hole was burned in the glass that surrounded the mountain. Dozens of multi-colored souls climbed through it to get inside. Spreading along the path, they shattered glass cabinets, broke the locks, and wrenched the lids and doors open.

"What are you doing?" I screamed.

A demure figure in a pristine white shroud ascended the path from the front entrance.

"Charity!"

"Madison?" She seemed surprised to see me, either not expecting to find me in the doorway to Avar's bedroom or not expecting to see me on the mountain at all.

"Did you know we were gone?" I guessed. It made perfect sense for her to break in while Avar and I were in Nerifir. I shook my head. "Why would you do something like this?"

She tilted her head with an accusing sigh. "Because you wouldn't do the right thing and help me, sweetie."

Glancing over her shoulder, she gently but firmly shoved me back into Avar's bedroom, entered after me, then closed the door behind her.

"How can breaking into someone's house be the right thing?" I exclaimed. "Look at the madness you've caused." I thrust a hand toward the closed door and the destruction that was happening behind it.

"None of the exhibits will be damaged or broken," Charity assured me hurriedly. "All will be returned to their rightful owners."

"But their rightful owners are dead, some for many centuries."

She was shorter than me, yet somehow still managed to stare me down. "Almost every item Avar has in his possession belongs to humanity, Madison. That's where we will take them all, back to the human world."

I paused, trying to consider the possible consequences her actions might have.

"It can go so wrong, Charity. Are you not afraid that the collection may fall into the wrong hands? Think about how much harm can be done with those weapon prototypes Avar has here. Or the chemical research he's acquired. Even if you don't start a war by dumping it all on humans now, trust me, there are a lot of unscrupulous assholes in my world who wouldn't hesitate to profit from hoarding the knowledge he has stored here and keeping the wealth it'll bring all to themselves. Oh, and don't even get me started on neglect. Do you know how sloppy humans can be at preserving their treasures? A huge chunk of Avar's collection still exists only because he rescued it before humans would've destroyed it."

Charity lifted her head in a dignifying gesture.

"As is their right," she said with aplomb.

"Do you mean you don't actually care if the treasures survive?"

"People created these exhibits, Madison. Without humans, this collection wouldn't exist in the first place. Whatever purpose they have created each item for, it is their right to either use it, lose it, or destroy it."

I stared at her, flabbergasted.

"But that's not *the right thing* to do, Charity. How can it be right?"

Charity embodied the virtue I deeply admired. It worried me that we didn't see eye to eye in this situation. All my life, I'd strived to be a good person. Did it mean I failed at that now?

She remained poised.

"People have the right to have what's theirs, and it's our duty to return it to them with the best intentions. After that, we can only hope that humanity has grown enough to choose their path wisely."

I scoffed at that.

"I'm afraid you don't know my kind very well. Or that you only see one side of humanity when there are so many."

"And what side do *you* see?" She squinted at me, taking in my torn, blood-stained tunic I kept pressing to my chest. "How evil do you think people are if you believe that my brother has a higher moral ground? Avaricia is the epitome of immorality." She frowned at my sorry state. "Madison, what did he do to you?"

She stepped around me to take a look at my back. I swiveled in the same direction to hide it from her, but it was too late, she saw the wounds and gasped. "You're hurt!"

"It's nothing," I protested.

"You're bleeding." She seemed genuinely appalled. "You're coming with me, Madison. I can't possibly leave you here for another minute."

"Avar didn't do it."

I realized how bad it looked to an outsider like Charity finding me in Avar's bedroom badly injured and in torn, dirty clothes.

"It happened in Nerifir," I tried to explain. "Avar would never hurt me."

"But he sent you to Nerifir, didn't he? What for? To get something for him? He'd stop at nothing to get what he wants. He's using you, poor thing. How can you be so blind as not to see it?"

"He's doing no such thing. We made a deal. I volunteered to go to Nerifir."

"Why do you defend him?" She peered at me closely, then shook her head with disappointment and regret. "Did his power and wealth corrupt you? Humans are highly susceptible to such things. But you can do better, Madison. Everyone can. Greed is powerful, but your free will can be stronger. You have to try to break free from him."

I huffed in frustration. "Charity, there is more to your brother than what you see. He's kind and caring. It's in his nature to take care of what he has, which includes his relationships with others. He keeps his distance from everyone because he gets attached too deeply and it hurts him to let go."

She looked at me with pity, shaking her head with a deep sigh.

"What a naïve little soul you are. Do you not know what my brothers are, Madison, how they came into existence? People took their worst fears, the most vile parts of the human character, the darkest, most shameful vices that no one would admit to having and named them *sins*. Then, they called the worst of them the Seven Mortal Sins. That's what my brothers are, my little human soul. They are the worst of the worst. You cannot embrace them. You have to defy them to preserve the good inside you. You must leave Avar. Please, help me fight him for you."

There wouldn't be much of a fight. I was about to leave Avar already, and he was not going to hold me anymore. Because of the deal we had made, he could let me go now without a threat to his existence. But I wasn't leaving for the reasons Charity wanted me to. I didn't see Avar as evil. It hurt me that someone else did, especially his own sister.

"You're judging him for what he *is*, instead of making an effort to understand what he *does*. There are good sides to Avar, just as there are better forms of greed. Frugality, prudence, conservation—all can be used for good."

She moved onto me, holding her finger up.

"Nothing about a sin can be good. Those who claim otherwise are tragically misguided or deeply corrupted. Which one are you, Madison? Do you want me to guide you out of your mistake? Do you wish to be saved? Or will you let greed claim you?"

I didn't feel "corrupted," but maybe that was the point? Fallen people didn't always realize how far they had fallen. Only there was nothing in Charity's idea of virtue that inspired me to follow her, either.

I met her judgmental stare with a smile.

"I love being claimed by him."

Charity pursed her lips, looking profoundly disappointed.

"Do you know how much evil is being done every day because of greed, human?"

"Just as much, I bet, as is done because of *the best intentions*," I retorted. "Now, if you'll excuse me, I need to find my favorite sin." I brushed by her and pushed the door open.

All hell had broken loose in Avar's usually quiet, peaceful, carefully organized dwelling. Cabinets stood wide open. The glass in many of them was smashed. Discarded empty crates and trunks rolled down the mountainside. Souls of all shapes and colors stuffed the huge sacks they'd brought with them with priceless treasures that Avar had collected and preserved for centuries.

The Sin of Greed himself stomped down the path. A bright

red glow pulsed through his chest with an intensity I'd never seen before—he was furious.

Lashing out with his tentacles, he grabbed every looting soul he passed.

"Get out of my place!" he thundered, ripping the half-filled bags out of their hands before tossing the souls out of the gaping hole in the glass.

He was terrifying in his rage.

"Just look at him." Charity sighed disapprovingly. "Is that who you choose to stand by?"

"Maddy." Avar saw me and rushed down the path, shoving the souls and broken display units out of his way. "Did anyone hurt you?" He crouched in front of me, his tentacles curling around me in a protective double hoop.

"No. I'm good," I assured him.

The red glow inside him fizzled out and died, calmed by the touch of my hand on his cheek.

"If anyone hurt her, it was *you*." Charity pointed an accusing finger at the wounds on my back.

Avar tightened his tentacles around me and rose to his feet, taking me along. He straightened to his full impressive height, placing me in the crook of his elbow.

"Leave, Charity," he growled. "And take all these misguided souls with you, unless you want me to toss all of you out through that hole."

Charity jerked her head high, pursed her lips, and marched by us as poised and proper as ever.

Avar glanced at the melting glass of the opening in the dome, then turned back to his sister.

"Charity," he called. "I believe you forgot to return something of mine."

She paused without turning around.

He stretched a tentacle in front of her. "My ward breaker?"

Without uttering a word, she searched in the folds of her shroud, then produced an elongated chrome cylinder with pewter designs etched into it.

Curling the end of his tentacle around the cylinder, Avar took it from her.

"Did E steal it for you?" he asked. "No one else has been here lately."

His sister didn't deign to reply. Holding her head high, she descended the path and departed. By then, most of the souls had already been gone. Some had been tossed out by Avar. Others had run out through the door or had climbed through the opening in the glass on their own. The few who remained scurried after Charity, leaving their bags behind.

I took a long look around the ransacked mountain.

"We have a mess to clean here now."

"*I* have a mess to clean. *You...*" He kissed the tip of my nose while adjusting my torn tunic over my shoulder. "You, my wounded kickass warrior, will have to rest and heal."

I smiled, leaning against his shoulder.

"I'm so not a kickass. Quite the opposite, really. I'd take the peace and quiet over a wild adventure any day."

"But you did so well during your adventure in Nerifir."

"Did I?" A warm pleasure spread through me at his praise. Apparently, I was guilty of the sin of pride too.

Avar brushed my tangled hair out of my face.

"You outwitted the High Lord's scouts."

"That wasn't hard to do," I chuckled. "Let's face it, those two weren't the sharpest knives in the drawer. There is a lot for them to work on in their next lives."

"You escaped the monster," he said, undeterred.

"I would not have done that without you. Escaping that thing was definitely our teamwork."

"And you saved the cat."

"*That* I did," I agreed, laughing. "I am taking full credit for that one."

As if on cue, Keeper sauntered toward us from wherever he'd been hiding during the attack on the mountain. One thing that the cat was really good at was hiding at the first sign of trouble. That was probably why he still had some of his nine lives left.

The cat rubbed his back on Avar's ankle.

"Is he asking for food?" Avar wondered.

"Probably."

"But I just fed him in the kitchen." He waved a tentacle up the path. "I gave him the rest of the taco meat you made the other day. I hope you don't mind. He seemed to like it."

"He sure likes food." I smiled.

Avar stared at the cat, looking lost in thought for a moment.

"Maddy, I think I can adjust the horologe, at least once, to manipulate time in the human world too. Would you like that? Would you like to return to the time when I took you? That way, you wouldn't have lost a day of your life at all."

"Would I still remember you and everything we have been through together?" I asked.

Would I still love you? I thought.

"Your memories are yours," he assured me. "No one can take them away. But now, you can stay here for a few more days to heal properly before you leave." He peered at me closely, as if trying to gauge my reaction. "I'm not asking you to stay for good, Maddy. Just to rest. For a few more days."

Like many people, I disliked long goodbyes. But I hated even more having to say goodbye to him at all.

Just a few more days...

"I'd love that, Avar."

16

Madison

A few days later

The air no longer smelled like lilacs when I woke up. It smelled like coffee. The sheets on my bed weren't lavender, either, but striped white-and-blue.

The wounds on my back had healed under Avar's care, and true to his word, he'd returned me exactly to the place and the time he had taken me from.

Our goodbye had lasted for several days while he was taking care of me. We cooked and had meals together, watching the sunset from our favorite room on top of his mountain. When my injuries got better, Avar made love to me with a poignant tenderness that filled me with both happiness and heartache.

When he finally brought me back to the alley behind the

restaurant, and it was time for us to part, I knew I had to make it quick before I lost my nerve and broke down.

"I'll never forget you," I said as he hugged me one last time.

"Nothing is forever," he replied.

"Not even goodbye?"

"Not even that."

"Will you wait for me, then?"

"For as long as it takes."

I didn't say I loved him, because I now had a lifetime to spend without him, and I couldn't live counting down the days until my death. I couldn't waste my years waiting for my life to be over. I had to make something of the life I got back.

Dishes clinked from the kitchen upstairs. Mom was up already. She'd gone to bed by the time I returned home last night.

I got up quickly, put some clothes on, and rushed upstairs to see her. At the entrance to the kitchen, I paused.

Mom raised me on her own. My grandma helped whenever she could, of course. But Mom had been my pillar of wisdom and strength when I was little. As a kid, I saw her tall and strong. But as I grew older, and she grew old, our roles had switched.

Now, I was taller and definitely stronger. Soon, it would be *me* taking care of *her*.

She turned away from the coffeemaker and found me watching her.

"Oh, you're up already?"

I swallowed a lump in my throat before hugging her. "I love you, Mom."

"I love you, too, baby." She chuckled when I wouldn't release her from the hug. "Did you have a bad dream or something? You're holding on to me the way you did when you were little and would wake up from a nightmare."

"A dream, yes," I agreed, finally letting go of her. "Only not really a bad one."

"Are you still okay driving me to the dentist this morning? If not, I should be fine on my own. It's just a local anesthesia, so—"

"I'll drive you." I kissed her cheek before reaching for a coffee cup. "I'm here, Mom. I can drive you anywhere you need."

"You're late," Claire accosted me the moment I entered the restaurant.

"Just by five minutes or so. I had to drive Mom to the dentist."

"Right. Well, I started prepping already."

"Thanks. I'll get to it too." I put away my purse and car keys in the drawer of the desk in the office, then changed my shoes and grabbed the apron before going to the kitchen.

"Is it okay if I leave after the lunch service?" Claire asked, getting out a carton of eggs to boil. "I'll try to be back before the dinner rush starts. Josh really wants those shoes."

"What shoes?" I carried a box of produce to the sink to wash.

She shrugged. "Some new trend in school. Everyone has them, so he wants some too. Did you bring the money?"

Now I remembered the conversation we had so long ago, it felt like in another lifetime. But for Claire, it'd just happened yesterday.

"Right. Well, about the money..."

Of course, I completely forgot to stop at the bank this morning. But maybe, it was a good thing that I did.

Until now, handing out money was my normal response in situations like these. I did it for the rush of the thrill of giving. Who didn't enjoy making people happy and seeing them smile and thank you for solving at least some of their problems that money could solve? I gave it to beat the guilt that would eat me alive if I didn't give. I gave because I could.

The problem was that I also impulsively gave even when I couldn't, when I had nothing to give and there was no money left to solve any of my own problems.

"What does Josh normally do after school?" I asked.

"What does he do?" She rolled her eyes. "He hangs out with his friends, plays video games, and eats a shitload of pizza. Why?"

"We could really use some help around here. If he came by after school for a few hours a couple of times a week, he'd earn enough to buy those shoes on his own."

She looked doubtful.

"Josh doesn't really want a job. He tried to shovel snow for money in the winter and hated it."

Why would Josh love to work if his mom always found a way to get him whatever he wished?

"Sooo..." Claire stretched the word tentatively. "Does that mean you're not lending me the money?"

I drew in a bracing breath.

"It means I'm not." I took out a loaf of bread to cut into croutons, avoiding Claire's disappointed stare. Saying "no" was hard, so hard, I would've rather cut my own tongue out. "You know what? Bring Josh over. I'll speak with him. Okay?"

"Okay." She didn't look convinced. But now, I had some time to prepare the speech to convince the little shit to get off his ass and get a job to help his mom out.

Simply giving her the money would've been so much easier. But that wasn't how I wanted to handle it anymore.

17

Avar

Dressed in black pants and a white blouse with her long, dark hair swept into an elegant bun, Maddy looked very different from the girl I knew in Purgatory who wore bright, breezy gowns and had windswept hair.

Collected and business-like, she peered at the screen of her tablet, then verified the box labels in the delivery truck parked in the alley behind her restaurant.

Hiding behind the stinky dumpster, I drank in every detail about her. No matter what she wore, she looked more beautiful than an angel to me because she was real—fragile, vulnerable, yet incredibly resilient when driven by a purpose.

Maddy held the door open for the delivery man to roll in the dolly with the boxes. As he entered the restaurant, just the two of us remained in the alley. She furtively glanced at the dumpster over her shoulder, as if stealing a moment from her reality to look into our past.

I shrank back, curling into a ball the size of a cat. It hurt to compress myself that much, but I couldn't risk Maddy spotting me. It wouldn't be fair of me to disrupt her life again. It wouldn't be fair to me to get the intoxicating pleasure of her attention only to give it up again. I had to be patient and wait.

Only waiting was getting increasingly harder to do, and coming here to catch glimpses of her didn't make it any easier.

The slam of the door behind her as she entered the restaurant was like a stab of a cold blade through my chest. Yet I already knew I'd be back again because *not* seeing her filled me with a much more excruciating pain than a stab of a blade.

Returning to my mountain didn't lessen the pain. It only increased the longing.

Keeper greeted me with a purr and a brush of his head against my ankle, then headed up the path to the kitchen, clearly expecting me to follow.

"I just fed you before I left," I reminded the cat, already knowing that he'd weasel a snack from me before dinner anyway. It was hard to stay firm with him as he got increasingly cuddlier the more I resisted. "Cute little bugger," I muttered, determined not to follow him to his food dish.

I once heard a saying during one of my past visits to the human world *"When parting from a loved one, the bigger burden falls on the one who stays."* It had never made more sense to me than it did now.

Maddy might be gone from Purgatory, but the memories of her remained on my mountain. My space was no longer my own. Anywhere I went, from the entrance at the bottom all the way up the spiral path to the very top, I was reminded of her.

The mountain trembled unexpectedly, alerting me to an uninvited visitor.

Maddy was right. A doorbell would've been less of a nuisance. But then again, with her gone, the visits to my mountain grew rare again. This was the first time someone had come over since her departure.

I opened the door and came face to face with Invi.

"What are you doing here?"

"Greetings to you, too, brother." He slithered in without waiting for an invitation.

I waited for all of his seemingly never-ending tail to get inside before closing the door.

"What do you want, Invi?"

"Do all visits need to have an agenda?"

"No. But yours usually have."

Realizing I wasn't following him up the path to the kitchen, Keeper turned back. At the sight of Invi, the cat hissed, puffed his tail, and hid behind my legs.

"What's *that?*" Invi stared at the animal.

"A cat." I lowered a tentacle and scratched behind Keeper's ear to calm him down. "Don't worry, Keeper. Invi looks scarier than he is. He doesn't eat cats. Frogs, maybe?"

Invi seemed too shocked to catch the barb. "Since when do you have a cat?"

"Since Madison brought him from Nerifir."

Keeper had become another constant reminder of her. I should've gotten rid of the creature long ago. Being a pet owner had never been my aspiration. But aside from the cat's unhealthy obsession with food, Keeper didn't bother me much. I'd made a small opening for him near the front door. He'd come and go as he pleased, roaming the mountainside and exploring the foothills at night, then sleeping in Maddy's room all day. Sometimes, he'd join me on the patio in the evening, his presence easing the loneliness of the sunset hour for me.

Invi's lips stretched into a grin that promised nothing good for me.

"You traded a woman for a cat?" he gloated.

"Fuck you." I turned to go up the path. "Don't let the door pinch your tail on the way out."

Of course, he didn't leave, following me up the mountain, instead. "Where are you going?"

"To feed the cat," I snapped. "I should get a dog next. A vicious one. To keep you off my property."

A dog wouldn't help. I'd have to trap and train a pack of werewolves to successfully guard my mountain against Invi's invasions. The bustard was fast and strong enough to probably move my mountain.

"You can't stay here all alone for decades now, Avar."

"Why not? It's not like you leave your swamp that often, either."

"Why would I leave it? It has everything I need."

"Yet here you are. You climbed all the way up here. What for?"

"Like I said, to keep you company, now that your human companion is gone."

I held my breath against a sharp pinch in my chest as we passed by Maddy's old room. Maybe I should've gotten rid of it. But I simply couldn't do it, clinging to every trace of her that I still had left.

Invi ran his gaze up the stairs to her old living space. The human sized table still stood in the middle with the few trinkets she'd found in my storage cave. I never finished clearing out the cave where we had worked together. Without her, loneliness reigned in there too.

"I can't believe you let her go." The accusation in Invi's voice poured anger over my pain, fanning my emotions into a flame.

I growled, my hands fisting at my sides, my tentacles lashing. Keeper jumped on one of them, trying to catch it, but missed, twisted in the air, and landed on all four paws.

Invi laughed.

"I can see how a pet can be entertaining."

I stroked the cat with the tip of my tentacle, then trailed it along the path, wiggling the tip.

Keeper crouched low to the ground, stalking the tentacle like a prey. As I dragged it past him, he jumped again, then rolled to his back, with the tip of my tentacle caught in his sharp claws.

I winced. If I had skin, it'd now be torn and bleeding. Keeper was cute but vicious, like all cats, I imagined.

"He likes to play." I petted Keeper's head before walking up the path again. He jumped to his paws, joining me on the way to the kitchen in hopes of getting a snack, no doubt.

Thanks to the cat, my anger at my brother dissipated. All that remained was a tendril of melancholy and the longing that never left.

"You won't understand, Invi, but I'll try to explain anyway. I love Madison. I love her so much that her pain hurts me, and her happiness makes me feel fulfilled. I didn't trade her for a cat like you say." I shook my head as he smirked. "I didn't even trade her freedom for a relic like she thinks I did. I bought her happiness, and I didn't care what it cost me, because it's the highest treasure of all."

We reached the top room, and Invi looked around the kitchen I'd built for Maddy. It remained intact as I had no heart to demolish, even as it was practically unusable for me with the counter height being just above my knee.

Thankfully, I didn't need to eat, and Keeper didn't care whether his food was cooked or raw. I cut a slice of meat and chopped it into smaller pieces for him.

Curling his tail under him, Invi watched me from the table where the belt that Maddy wore on her trip to Nerifir still lay. I hadn't completely emptied it yet, fearing the memories and the emotions it would bring. Ever since Maddy and I returned from Nerifir, it'd been nothing but a whirlwind of emotions.

"They say love can bring the highest pleasure," Invi said. "Looking at you now, brother, I would argue it can bring the deepest sorrow too. Was it all worth it in the end? Falling in love only to lose it like that?"

Was it worth it?

Were the brief moments of intense pleasure when Maddy was close to me worth the decades of solitude suspended in wait now that she was gone? Would I have done it all over again if I knew how it'd all end?

"Yes," I said. "I'd give everything I have for just a moment of the true happiness that Maddy gave me. It's worth it all and more."

Folding his arms across his chest, Invi gaped at me.

"You, the Sin of Greed, would *give?*"

I nodded confidently without a hint of regret about the choices I'd made.

"It'd be a fair trade for me."

Indi didn't stay long. I let him make his way down to the exit on his own while I picked up Maddy's belt from the table and emptied its pockets and pouches.

A pale blue stone fell onto the table next to the stuffed snake. I didn't remember packing the stone and lifted it to my eyes for a better look.

Having finished his food, Keeper sauntered past me, probably on his way to Maddy's bedroom for a nap. The sunlight glistened in the gears on his collar. The polished moonstone between the gears remained pale in the sunlight. It glowed its brightest on a full moon night, when its magic was the strongest, strong enough to allow a goddess to live in the world of the mortals.

I turned the stone from Maddy's belt between my fingers.

Did she bring it from Nerifir and forgot to tell me? A lot had happened upon our return. I didn't even put everything away right after as I usually try to do. Had I even locked the transcendence potion properly? I couldn't remember.

The delicate, shimmering moonstone was beautiful even in the daylight. And I wondered whether its power could do for a sin what it'd done for a goddess.

18

Madison

"Who is doing the soup kitchen delivery this week?" I asked, going through the next week's order form on my computer.

The door to my office was open. Claire stood in the doorway with the evidence of wilted cilantro in her outstretched hand.

"Josh is," she said. "He's coming straight after school by bike, and I have the trailer loaded for him already."

"Good. Tell him to stop at the store on the way back to get some fresh cilantro. Get the money from the till and bring me the receipt."

"Will do, boss." Claire gave me a mock solute with a good-natured smile before departing to execute the new plan.

There had been a few small but important changes at the restaurant over the past month.

The day I refused to finance the purchase of his coveted shoes, Claire dragged Josh in here and let me present my offer to him personally. Somehow, I managed to convince the boy to take the job on a trial basis. He still threatened to quit every single shift. But he bought his shoes last week and still stuck around after that, probably having another purchase in mind already.

I never ordered the overpriced present for Sam's second cousin whom I'd never met. But I gave him another paid day off to sleep in and rest after the wedding.

Quitting charity had never been my plan. I loved giving. I just gave in a more organized way now. I scheduled and budgeted my donations and recorded every transaction, mindful of such boring things as tax deductions.

I didn't just need to keep this restaurant afloat, I was determined to make it thrive.

In Purgatory, I let Greed claim me, and on Earth, I learned frugality. If my business failed, the people I loved would suffer from its failure. I had to succeed to be in a better position to help them too.

After finishing the order forms, I locked my desktop and went to the kitchen.

Lee, my best cook, had been promoted to Head Chef, which left me with more time to focus on the business and the creative side of running a restaurant. I hired a new sous chef to help Lee. And now, we were open all seven days of the week, including Mondays.

It'd been only a month. The restaurant wasn't making much of a profit yet. I still lived with my mom with no chance of getting my own place anytime soon. But we broke even and moved into the black this month, and my confidence in our future was stronger than ever.

With Lee managing the kitchen, I was able to finally take a day off to go to a spa with my mom last week. Seeing that I now might have some time to date again, Claire had renewed her offer to set me up with her neighbor.

In my mind, I agreed that I probably should. I still had a whole life ahead of me. I couldn't keep putting it on hold. I had to date, build relationships, maybe start a family one day...

Except that I couldn't get the sweet air of Purgatory out of my lungs and the memories of Avar's gentle touch out of my head. I missed the scent of lilacs and the taste of grapes. I missed the view of the sunset from the patio off Avar's kitchen. I even missed Keeper and had already scheduled a donation to an animal shelter in his honor next month.

All this time, Avar never came to see me. He'd never said that he would. We'd made no such promises when we parted. I knew he wanted to give me space to build a life on my own in a world where he couldn't be with me. Maybe he also knew that a visit wouldn't be enough, that once he saw me, we wouldn't be able to let go of each other. But understanding it didn't make me miss him any less.

Sam grabbed a full garbage bag and headed through the back door to the alley. I resisted the urge to volunteer to do it for him. I'd run into that alley way too many times, hoping to find someone who wasn't there, searching for the purple glow between the dumpsters against any common sense, and of course, never finding it.

The back door closed. I walked into the fridge and focused on its contents, taking notes on my tablet for replenishment orders.

"Hey, Maddy?" Sam returned from the alley and poked his head into the walk-in fridge. "There's a delivery truck in the back. When the garbage truck comes by, the guys will be pissed that he's blocking their way. I told him to move, but the driver said he has a delivery for you."

I left the fridge and closed the door behind me.

"I'll take care of him."

"Make sure you do." Sam winked at me. "The guy is hot as sin."

The tablet nearly slipped from my fingers. I set it on the worktable carefully lest I drop it.

"What did you say?"

"I said I'd climb him like a tree, girl." He grinned.

Lee cast Sam a glance from behind the stove. "Don't you have a boyfriend?"

"I do," Sam agreed. "That's why Maddy needs to hit on this guy. Honestly, someone *needs* to hit on that."

"Hit on what?" Claire entered the kitchen from the dining room.

Lee rolled his eyes. "The truck driver with the delivery in the back. Sam is looking for someone to fuck him."

Claire snorted a laugh, then stared at Lee with alarm.

"Are you saying there is a truck in the back? Right now? But it's garbage day. Mo will throw a fit when he gets here."

"I'll deal with it," I repeated, opening the back door and heading out into the alley.

The delivery truck was parked badly, blocking not just the driveway to the dumpsters but also the biking path that crossed the alley near the street.

The driver waited for me at the truck's back door. He was tall. One might really need to climb him to even reach for a kiss. He was big too. His wide shoulders barely had enough space in his checkered red flannel shirt. Sam was right about his looks too. From what I could see between his dark baseball hat and the full chestnut-brown beard, the man was handsome.

At the sight of me, he took his hands out of the pockets of his jeans and shifted his weight from one foot clad in a hiking boot on to another.

His outfit of a stereotypical lumberjack seemed to have

come straight from some old sitcom, except for a large moonstone ring on his right hand. The ring appeared to belong more to a fantasy movie or a museum and clashed with the casual lumberjack vibe he seemed to be going for. I noticed he held no electronic signature pad or a waybill paperwork for me to sign.

"Hi," I greeted since he didn't say a word, just staring at me. "I think we're done with deliveries for today. Are you sure it's not a mistake? Do you have the right address?"

His beard parted with a smile in a way that felt eerily familiar.

"No mistake. For the first time in a month, I am exactly where I want to be, Maddy."

My heart tightened at the sound of his familiar voice, then blossomed like a garden in spring. Everything inside me turned light and airy. I didn't remember how I made the few steps to close the distance between us.

"You?" I reached up to touch his cheek.

He towered over me, but at his current human height, I could reach his face without asking him to lift me. His eyes crinkled in the corners, his smile shining through their vivid violet hue.

"Every fucking night," he murmured, "I've been dreaming about kissing you again."

"Avar..." I curled my fingers in his beard, pulling him down to me.

His arm, not a tentacle, wrapped around my waist as he swept me off my feet for a kiss. He still smelled like lilacs and tasted sweeter than grapes. I closed my eyes, allowing my memory to transport me back to his mountain.

"I've waited for you," I murmured against his lips. "I knew I shouldn't, but I wanted to see you again so badly."

"I have come here. Many times."

"When? Why didn't I see you?"

"I came during the day, so my glow would be easier to hide."

"Why did you hide?"

"I didn't want to disturb the life you had to build without me. But I couldn't stay away from you, Maddy. I had to know you were safe and well. I didn't want you to see me unless it was acceptable for everyone else to see me too. And now, it is."

"But how?" I stroked along his hard jawline, feeling every strand of his beard under my fingers. Worry slithered in my chest next. "Avar, where did you steal this body?"

It was a great body, too, I could tell by the strong hold of his thick arms around me, the sharp cut of his jaw under the beard, and the hard feel of his muscles under that soft flannel shirt.

"*Steal?*" he chuckled. "Is that what you think of me?"

"Just tell me, please, that the soul who occupied it before you vacated it without your help."

"My dear sweet Maddy, this body is all my own. No soul has ever had it before me. And I have you to thank for it." He lifted his hand with the ring to show it to me. "I found this stone in one of the pockets of the belt you wore to Nerifir."

Now I recognized the stone as the one I took from Ghata's shrine in the monastery.

"Oh, I completely forgot about it."

The purple sparkles that hadn't been there before flashed behind the milky-blue surface of the stone.

"I found out that werewolves used the power of moonlight stored in stones like this one to give Ghata her physical shape. After some research and with a few modifications, I was able to use the stone's magic to create a body for me too."

I slid a hand down his wide chest.

"It turned out very well, I have to say."

He beamed.

"You like it?"

"You've always looked *hot as sin*, darling," I quoted Sam and confessed, "I love you, Avar. All of you, not just the body."

I lifted my eyes to see his reaction.

He held his breath for a moment, as if absorbing the words I'd just said.

"That means I can make my confession, too, then." He hugged me tightly, lifting me off the ground. "I love you, Maddy, more than I've ever loved any soul before, more than I've ever loved anyone as long as I've lived."

Happiness grew inside me so big, I feared I'd float up into the sunny skies. I wrapped my arms around his neck to hold on.

He kissed me, cupping my cheeks, and I realized those weren't his arms that held me above the ground. A pair of glowing tentacles wound tightly around me, holding me to him.

"Sorry, I didn't mean for those to slip out." Avar laughed, replacing the tentacles with his arms around me and making the tentacles disappear. "I promise not to let it happen again when other humans are around."

"It'd be really hard to explain them otherwise," I laughed. Raking my fingers through his beard, I kissed his lips, his cheeks, then the tip of his nose. "How are we going to do it, Avar? Will you stay here with me?"

"I can stay here. Or you can come with me. I don't care, as long as we're together."

Now that we both could live in either world, there was no need for us to ever be apart.

"We can do both. I have more help to run the restaurant now. And you can look after your collection from here, too, right? The commute to Purgatory isn't too bad."

He nodded. "Definitely easier than getting through the traffic in this city."

"Did you drive this truck here yourself? Did you learn how to drive?"

"I've learned many new things lately, dearest. Even how to be a cat owner."

"How is Keeper? Will you bring him here too?"

"He wouldn't come here," Avar chuckled. "The cat is at Gul's right now. The rascal loves it there with all the food, and Gul always appreciates having someone to feed."

He gave me another kiss before pulling away.

"I've got something for you."

"A present?" I smiled, glancing at the truck. "Where did you get this truck, anyway?"

"I have my sources," he replied enigmatically, shoving the truck doors open.

A huge sparkle of purple fireflies burst out into the alley.

It was a nice sunny day, but in the shadows from the tall buildings in the alley, the glowing fireflies looked like stars swarming around us in a twister.

"This is beautiful!" I tipped my face up, laughing.

Avar looked perplexed, however. "How did they get there?"

"You didn't plan it? This isn't a part of your gift?"

"No. They must've crawled into the boxes when I brought them outside. I certainly didn't plan to bring them here all the way from Purgatory." Avar was far too practical for grand gestures like this. Then he saw my smile. "But now I'm glad I did, since you like it so much."

"I do." I lifted my hand for one of the fireflies to rest on it for a moment.

It sparkled like gemstone before taking off into the air again. I followed it back to the truck. Trunks, crates, baskets, and boxes piled up high inside it.

"What's that? Avar, are you decluttering?"

Standing next to me, he hugged my shoulders with one arm.

"I went through my collection, Maddy, thinking about what

would make you happy the most. And well, this one here..." He opened a tall cabinet.

Inside was a stand with a contraption that reminded me of a skeleton, with a spine, arm bones, a ribcage, and hip support, as well as the long, thin braces for legs. All parts were delicately constructed, which made the entire piece look like jewelry.

"Is that..." I stopped, unsure of my guess. The piece looked more like an adornment than a device.

"Yes, it's the prototype I retrieved from the dumpster the night I met you."

"*Met* me? You took me," I corrected.

"I did. And I can't regret it even if I tried. I need you, Maddy. I need you to be mine."

I wrapped my arm around his back, bringing us closer, and hooked a thumb in the waistband of his jeans. Avar was wearing jeans. Who thought I'd ever get to see that?

"There is more here." He opened the trunks, shoved the baskets closer, and removed lids from the boxes. "I have some medical research here to help people fix their current bodies, since you believe they shouldn't wait until their next life to enjoy this world. When I think about how happy you make me, I want everyone to be happy, too. Here are some rare gemstones that can be traded for money if you wish. And this is a very promising research on an alternative source of energy. Shoes and pieces of clothing made in a technique that modern humans never heard of. And these here are some scrolls from the warehouse of the Library of Alexandria—"

"You're returning them?" I gasped.

"Just some plays and poems for now. I need to see what humans do with them before I consider parting with the rest."

"But how are you giving it all up, Avar? You can't *give*. You trade. What are you getting in exchange for all these treasures?"

Holding me close, he brushed a strand of hair away from my face.

"I've discovered the biggest treasure of all, Maddy. To me, it's worth more than any precious stones or any fortune in existence. It's your happiness. There is nothing I wouldn't give for it. If this is what you want..." He gestured at the truck. "Then it's yours. All I ask in exchange is your smile."

I couldn't hold it back even if I tried. The biggest, brightest smile sprang to my lips, uncontainable.

"There it is," he murmured approvingly. "My biggest reward."

He lowered his mouth to mine, and I met him in a kiss. My head was spinning at the thought that I was kissing Avar again, that after weeks of dreaming about him and missing him, I could finally call him mine.

"Wow!" A gasp came from the back door of the restaurant.

I let go of Avar reluctantly to find Claire watching us kiss inside the slow twirl of the fireflies.

"So..." She scratched the side of her nose, giving Avar a long once-over. "Mo is here to pick up the garbage, and he's throwing a fit about the access to the dumpster being blocked. He couldn't even walk around here to tell you to move because of the way your truck is parked. You're blocking the entire alley, buddy."

As far as I knew, they didn't give driving lessons in Purgatory. I had no idea how Avar managed to drive this truck at all, let alone back it in.

"Also..." Claire finally tore her attention from Avar and moved it to me. "I didn't think you'd take Sam's request to climb a stranger quite so literally. Though, I always suspected you had a thing for truck drivers, even when you wouldn't let me set you up with Tony."

I smoothed my hair and adjusted my blouse.

"Claire, this is Avar. He isn't exactly a stranger. We've met before."

"It is a pleasure to meet you." Avar inclined his head in an elegant bow that made his outfit look even more out of place.

"Ooh." Claire's face lit up. "You have a secret lover?"

"Not so secret, anymore." Avar found my hand and linked our fingers. "We're dating."

"You are?" She moved her eyes from him to me.

I squeezed his hand, unable to stop smiling.

"Yes, we are."

A loud, angry honking came from the street. Mo was a nice guy in every way. The one thing he always lacked, however, was patience.

"We'll have to move the truck," I said as Avar locked the trailer's door. "We'll take it to my house, for now. Then we'll figure out the best thing to do with each item. Claire, I'm taking the rest of the day off. Lee can manage the dinner service without me tonight."

She nodded but didn't leave. Leaning with her shoulder against the door frame, she watched Avar and me with a little stunned but happy smile.

I turned to my mortal sin.

"I'm taking you home, Avar. You're going to meet my mom. Just a word of warning. She'll adore you. So, get ready to be adored."

He smiled at me, unconcerned.

My boyfriend. The Sin of Greed.

How would I ever be able to explain this to anyone?

It was a good thing that I had no intention of explaining anything. As long as we were together, it was all that mattered.

Epilogue

Madison

A month later

I opened my eyes to the bright morning light flooding the room through the window of our bedroom. Avar forgot to hide his horns last night. As he tucked his face against my shoulder, the purple glow of a horn shone straight into my eye.

It was late morning already, but he still looked deep asleep, and I didn't want to wake him. Yesterday was our moving day, and he'd worked hard carrying twice as many boxes as any human could lift.

I'd finally moved out of my mom's house, sooner than I'd ever thought I would. Avar and I had found a cute apartment in a low-rise about halfway between my restaurant and Mom's place. He insisted on making the down payment since he now lived in my world just as much as in Purgatory, if not more. I agreed because the slowly but steadily increasing profits from the restaurant finally made a mortgage look affordable to me.

I'd been back to his mountain a few times in the past month. With no commute time, it was even easier to visit than if he lived across the street. The only downside was that I always passed out on the way to Purgatory. That was the consequence of bringing a living body to the world of the dead.

We'd also been carefully researching the best places to donate each of Avar's treasures that he'd brought back to our world. So far, we'd been able to give away almost half of them already.

Avar's beard tickled my arm. He refused to shave it, claiming that a bare chin would make him feel uncomfortable. I didn't mind. I loved his beard, whether it was hair or feelers.

His dark chestnut locks fell over his forehead. I moved them aside carefully and gently kissed his temple. I hated to wake him up, but Avar's brother Gul, the Sin of Gluttony, invited us for brunch today, and we both decided it was finally time for me to meet his extraordinary family. We couldn't sleep in this morning, or we'd be late. And it'd be rude to show up late for my first meeting with Avar's brothers.

I kissed his temple again, then his forehead, then the base of his horn. He made a soft sound deep inside his throat and stirred.

Sticking my tongue out, I slowly dragged it along the entire length of the front horn that was closest to me.

He rolled to his back with a low moan and stretched through his entire body, still keeping his eyes closed.

I ran my tongue in a circle around his horn, then wrapped my lips around the pointy tip and sucked gently.

"Fuck..." he exhaled, betraying the fact that he was very much awake now.

His back arched. The sheet tented over his crotch with his erection. His horns were his sinful place, and I loved that.

Wrapping my hand around one of his horns, I peppered kisses down his face, neck, and chest before reaching under the blanket.

Avar preferred to sleep in the nude. His erection sprang into my hand, and it was almost as hard as his horn. Thankfully, in his human form, his dick was a much more manageable size that I could take in any way I liked.

Kissing his chest, I caressed both his cock and his horn.

He grunted, snapping his arms around me. His tentacles extended from his sides, grabbing me in an inescapable hold.

He growled, rolling me onto my back.

"Well, I'm awake now."

"Morning, darling." I smiled, reaching into the drawer of my nightstand for a condom.

In his human form, Avar's orgasm was also human in every way, with no light show, but with a very real chance of ending up in a pregnancy that we weren't ready for yet.

He rolled the condom on, playfully jerking up an eyebrow, then buried his face between my breasts. His corollas fluttered down my arms, scattering light, gentle kisses over my skin and fanning my desire.

A moan escaped my lips. I opened my legs, and Avar lost no time slipping a hand between my thighs. His fingers quickly found my clit throbbing hot with need. He kissed down my breast, then sucked the nipple into his mouth, gently rolling it between his teeth.

Pleasure rolled through me in a swell. With Avar, there was never any need for the cursed collar. He always managed to make me crazy with lust, using only the magic of his touch.

"How much do you want me, Maddy? Tell me," he demanded.

"More than anything. I want you more than anything in the world and always will."

Possession was the very nature of the Sin of Greed. The loss of what he had was his worst fear. Since I'd become Avar's biggest treasure, even the idea of losing me terrified him. It was a good thing that I loved being his, fully and completely.

"You have me, Avar, and you always will. I love you, and I'm not going anywhere."

"I love you, too, my treasure. More than anything in this world or any other."

He entered me slowly, savoring the sensation of our connection. His thrusts quickly grew more desperate. My need for him grew too. I wrapped my legs around his middle. The tip of his tentacle pressed to my clit, teasing me with an approaching orgasm. His other tentacle slipped between me and the sheets from the back, circling my back entrance.

Heat spiked in me. Pleasure crested. My mouth fell open as my eyes closed. He swallowed my moans with a kiss, joining me in climax. We rode the waves of pleasure together, and I didn't release him from my embrace even after.

He kept holding me, too, his face buried in my shoulder.

"Are you sure you want to spend your only day off this week with my family?" he murmured against my skin. "Or could I possibly persuade you to spend it just like this? In bed, with me?"

"Tempting." I smiled. Doing anything with Avar was my favorite pastime. Spending the whole day in bed with him sounded fantastic. "But Gul has been inviting us for weeks, and we finally agreed. It'd be really rude not to show up now."

"He'd get over it," he muttered grumpily. Then sighed heavily, probably remembering that he was way too old for a tantrum. "Fine. Let's get ready." He climbed out of bed. "But we're taking a shower together. And I demand the right to wash you."

"Then we'll definitely be late." I laughed as he hauled me into the bathroom, his corollas already plucking at my nipples again and his fingers straying too far around my thigh.

"It's the price I'm willing to pay," he declared, turning on the shower. "Trust me, we deserve this today before meeting my brothers. They can be extremely aggravating."

Avar and I walked hand in hand from his mountain in Purgatory. He still wore his ring that kept him in his human form. It was easier for us to walk side by side this way.

In his other hand, Avar carried a basket with two bottles of wine and a platter of canapés I made for Gul's brunch.

We took the narrow road that ran around the town and into the fields where Gul's house stood. It was a sprawling one-story building with a wraparound porch and white railings. Made of thick yellow logs, the house had a red roof with corners curved up like in Chinese pagodas. The tall contraption above looked like a bell tower with a gazebo on top and a bunch of gothic turrets.

"This is the most confusing construction in terms of style," I noted.

Avar shrugged. "Gul would never let the limitations of just one style hold him back in his indulgence."

Despite the seemingly random assembly of architectural elements, Gul's house didn't look ugly. It seemed to be a happy place, surrounded by a field of blooming sunflowers, and I instantly regretted not accepting Gul's invitation earlier.

The entrance opened into a spacious room with lots of comfy seating and a large screen in a crystal frame on the wall above the fireplace. A rerun of *Friends* playing on the screen was dubbed in a language that sounded Italian with what looked like Korean subtitles on the bottom. The sins wouldn't care about the language, of course, since they understood them all.

The room was empty.

"Is that the TV?" I asked, pointing at the screen. "Pandora's box?"

"Yes." Avar nodded. "Mother's gift."

A rustling sound of something shifting along the floor came from behind me.

"Hi, Invi," Avar greeted. His tentacle immediately whipped around me, forming a protective circle.

Apprehension slithered into my chest as I turned around. The shape of the sin entering the room was humanoid, but the wavering outline of it betrayed that it'd been something else just a moment ago. The outline settled into the green glowing shape of a handsome man with long, hunter-green hair.

"Hello, Madison," he said in a deep, melodious voice that I recognized.

"We've met before. Kind of.... You were there the day I was taken... I mean, when Avar took me from the alley." I offered him my hand. "It's nice to finally meet you face to face and under much better circumstances."

"It's a real pleasure to see you again." Instead of shaking my hand, Invi bowed gracefully and placed a kiss on it.

Not expecting the gesture, I glanced at Avar, who worked his jaw in annoyance.

"Invi's manners are outdated," he explained. "He doesn't come to the human world often."

"And who is to blame for that?" Invi retorted, releasing my hand. "If Avar didn't hoard the transcendence potion—"

"You'd follow me on every trip and grab twice as much of anything I take," Avar finished for his brother.

A red streak of irritation flashed through Invi's emerald shape.

"Where is everyone?" I changed the subject to ease the tension.

"Out in the yard." Invi waved a hand at the open patio doors. "Gul sent me inside to get more lemonade."

"Do you need help?" I asked.

Avar took my hand. "He'll be fine."

"Thank you, Madison. I'll manage on my own." Invi bowed to me politely. "Welcome to the family. I'm looking forward to getting to know you better."

"The fuck you will," Avar gritted though his teeth as Invi headed through an arched exit into what looked like a ginormous kitchen in the middle of Gul's farmhouse.

I jerked Avar's hand. "Hey. He's being nice to us."

"To *you*," he corrected. "He is being exceptionally nice to *you*, Maddy. To me, Invi is just being envious, like he often is. He always wants what others have. Just look at him." He gestured in the direction where his brother had departed. "He isn't even in his own form. He'd rather look like someone else than himself."

According to Avar, Invi often took the siblings' rivalry to a whole new level. But he was the Sin of Envy. Competition was expected from someone like him. Personally, I found Invi's flair of old-fashioned charm endearing.

"He must have his reasons for taking a different form," I said in his defense.

Shaking his head, Avar led me out of the patio doors.

"Well, there are more where Invi comes from. Are you

ready to meet the rest of my brothers? Or should we go home before it's too late?"

Avar might not speak about his brothers kindly, but I knew he thought them safe. He would never bring me to this place otherwise.

When I glanced at the group gathered for brunch, however, my apprehension surged higher.

Gul's yard was a large clearing in the sunflower field. It was set up like an outdoor living room, with wicker furniture, several gazebos, a firepit, and a huge outdoor kitchen.

Five giant, monstrous forms lounged around, with a golden yellow one standing by the grill. The mouth-watering aroma of marinated grilled meat wafted over the field, reaching the house.

"They are..." I swallowed hard, taking in all their tails, wings, hooves, and horns...so many horns.

"Monsters?" Avar finished for me. "That's right. They are monsters." He took the magical moonstone ring off his finger and placed it into a candy dish under Pandora's box. "But so am I, Maddy. I'm a monster too."

His human form turned transparent. The purple glow burst through his disappearing clothes. Tentacles and feelers unfurled. Horns sprouted. He grew, turning into the monster he truly was, but I loved every horrifying part of him.

"Whatever comes, I'll protect you, Maddy. Even from my own family." He wrapped a supportive tentacle around me, then handed me the basket with wine and canapés. "Here. You made these. Do you want to give them to Gul yourself? He's the yellow one by the grill."

I nodded, taking the basket from him.

Gul and Sup, the Sins of Gluttony and Pride, had helped Avar to take care of me during my early days in Purgatory.

They fed and clothed me. I already met Invi, the Sin of Envy. And I loved the Sin of Greed, madly.

The seven deadly sins weren't as bad as the world had made them out to be. One just needed to look deeper to find the good side of each.

"I'm ready." Gripping the basket, I stepped out into the yard. "Let's meet them all."

Patreon

A NSFW illustration to Chapter 7 scene—where Madison gets herself in a predicament after trying on the cursed collar and Avar very gallantly helps her out of the situation—is posted on the author's Patreon, available to patrons of all tiers:

Next in Seven Horny Sins
Let Me Win You

Invi

From around the corner of the building, I scanned the crowd that gathered in front of the dance hall...um, no, they called it "a night club or just "a club" nowadays. I had to remember that.

I shook my head, both annoyed and frustrated. Humans changed their language just as often as they changed their clothes. It was hard to keep up, especially if one came to this world only once in several decades like I did.

My brother Avar, the Sin of Greed, kept under lock both the transcendence potion needed to travel to the humans' world and the moonstone ring that gave one a physical body. Through careful planning and a little luck, I'd managed to acquire both now and came here to find *her*, the human woman who'd love me the way Madison loved Avar.

From what I'd learned about modern humans from watching their movies on the Pandora's box home in Purgatory, the best way to meet a woman was to "go out." A night club was a suitable place for that.

The crowd at the front door formed a long line that curved into the alley from the main street. The club was the latest "it spot" in the city, and every eligible bachelor and bachelorette appeared to strive to get in tonight.

A car pulled over from the busy street, and a couple exited. Pulling his female companion by her hand, the man confidently strolled to the door.

"I'm Sabine's friend," he said to the guard at the entrance.

Not slowing down, the man then sauntered through the door, leading his woman along.

"Do you have an invitation?" the guard yelled after the couple.

But the pulsing lights and the music from the inside had already swallowed them both.

I could walk all the way to the end of the line and spend an hour or two waiting to get in. Time was of no essence to me. But from what I'd learned, women appreciated confidence.

Here, in this unfamiliar world with its strange scents and sounds, feeling confident wasn't easy. But I had mastered the art of imitation better than anyone.

Rolling back my shoulders, I smoothed a hand over my hair that the barber had spent a considerable amount of time to trim and style into a deliberately messy knot on the back of my head, assuring me that was the most dashing way to wear long hair nowadays.

I unzipped my tailored leather jacket, just like the man who'd just entered the club wore his. The dark shirt I wore underneath and the black pants were rather plain for my tastes, but I chose the clothes after carefully studying the current fashion trends. All pieces came from famous fashion houses and cost me a small fortune in gems and gold I'd traded for the modern paper currency for shopping. But humans valued their appearances, and first impressions were important.

Heaving a breath, I stepped out from the shadows and into the lights of the electric lanterns on the street.

The guard at the door was talking to the young woman who was first in line, and I walked past them like the other man had, as if I expected to enter without being stopped, as if I had every right to be inside.

"Um, sir?" the guard made a move my way.

"I'm a friend of Sabine's." I waved him off with an indulging smile, graciously forgiving him for his mistake of trying to stop me.

"Are you on the list?" His words almost drowned in the noise and music blasting from the inside.

I nodded, not slowing down. The guard, the line, and the street were already behind me. The foul air of the night club engulfed me, rich with body odor, perfume, alcohol, and a trace of rodent droppings.

In front of me lay a room filled with humans, with one of them destined to become what Madison now was for my brother Avar.

Madison was supposed to be mine. I saw her first. But the greedy asshole that he was, Avar grabbed her before I got a chance.

For a while, I'd plotted to take her from him. I'd imagined she'd see me as her rescuer and favor me over him.

Sadly, Madison fell in love. Who knew it'd take her such a short time to form a deep affection for my grumpy, anti-social, void of any charisma brother? But she did, and I was too late. I missed my chance. If I took her away from him now, she'd despise me.

"Hey," one of the group of men next to me elbowed his buddy. "Wanna hear a joke?" He didn't wait for his friends' replies and kept talking, "So, two chicks die and get to the purgatory, and the ground there is solidly covered with ducks."

Ducks?

Why ducks?

It made no sense. There aren't that many ducks in Purgatory. Some live in my swamp, but there aren't that many that would cover the entire ground.

I paused to hear more. My world had been created through humans' beliefs. If enough people believed in this duck nonsense, we risked for this story to become our reality. I winced, not looking forward to ducks invading my home.

Taking a swig of his beer, the man continued, barely containing his excitement, "An angel tells the girls not to step on a duck or they'll be punished. One of them steps on a duck by mistake and a butt-ugly dude appears, chained to her arm for the rest of eternity. The other one is super careful and doesn't step on any ducks for a year. Then one day... Poof! A hot guy is chained to her wrist—"

His buddies snickered before he even reached the end of the joke. And the man was practically choking on laughter and beer as he delivered the punchline.

I pondered the joke. Was it supposed to be funny? Humor was a peculiar thing, just as unique to a person as their hair or eye color.

Sweeping the room with my gaze, I realized I was searching for a dark-haired woman. Madison had dark-brown hair, almost black.

I realized it wasn't exactly Madison that I was the most envious of my brother about. More than anything, I just wanted what she and Avar had together. But this was the city where she lived. The club was just around the corner from the restaurant that she owned. Somehow, it all felt like a good point to start searching for that special human woman of my own.

As the music dipped with one song ending and before the

other one began, a burst of laughter broke through. It was loud, musical, and filled with the happiness I longed for.

I pivoted toward the sound as did almost everyone else in the place, all of us staring at a young woman at the table in the corner. Faced with the attention, her laughter tapered to a most adorable giggle. She threw her hand over her mouth, the humor now bouncing only in her eyes.

Before I even realized what I was doing, I headed toward her table.

"Good evening, fair ladies," I greeted the woman and her female companion who was sharing the table with her.

The object of my attention peered at me, her hazel-green eyes narrowing in suspicion. Then a new spark of humor burst in them as she lowered her hand and gave me a cordial smile.

"Good evening to you, too, mighty knight," she matched my tone. "What brings you to our neck of the woods this fine evening?"

She clearly was mocking me, but I couldn't even muster any offense in response, wishing to hear her laugh, even if at my expense.

"I heard you laughing," I replied sincerely.

She blinked, gentle blush spreading on her round cheeks.

"It was rather loud, wasn't it?" She bit her lip.

"Nicole loves to laugh," her companion, a blonde young woman with delicate facial features, stated. "It can't be helped."

"I like that." I ran a hand over my hair and confessed, "I'd love to hear you laugh again."

Humor shone brighter in her eyes. They weren't brown like Madison's, I noted. In fact, Nicole looked nothing like Madison. Her auburn-red hair was lighter. Her body was plumper with far more curves. It was hard to accurately gauge her height while she was sitting, but she seemed shorter than Madison too.

None of it mattered, however. I said I wished to hear her laugh again, and I wholeheartedly meant it.

"Make me laugh, then," she challenged. "Say something funny."

Her companion rested her chin in her hand, her elbow propped on the table. "Tell us a joke, stranger."

"A joke?"

My mind drew blank. It was hard to muster words when they both stared at me expectantly. The stakes of making a good impression rose exponentially the longer I gazed into Nicole's green eyes with gold and brown flecks.

"Yes." She nodded. "Do you know any?"

After millennia of existence, all I could remember at that moment was one single joke. It floated on the surface of my mind like a fucking duck.

"Two women died and went to Purgatory..." It was a mistake. The joke was stupid. It'd ruin any chance I had with Nicole. But she expected me to speak, so I pulled a chair from the table and sat down to get closer and make myself heard over the music. "Let me assure you, there aren't that many ducks in Purgatory. Animal spirits travel freely between worlds, taking whatever shape they wish. But in this particular version of the afterlife, apparently, the ground is covered with ducks—"

Nicole laughed. And I stopped, mesmerized by the sound and the sight of dimples gracing her cheeks.

"Shh." Her companion tapped on Nicole's hand. "Let him finish, Nic."

"Go on." Nicole graciously gestured for me to continue. She pressed her lips, trying to contain her laugh, and I took it as a challenge, longing to set it free again.

"One woman accidentally steps on a duck, and she is immediately chained to a man of a hideous appearance as a punishment. The other woman managed to avoid such a misfortune for a year. Upon which a handsome man appears, chained to her wrist. 'Are you my reward for me being careful all this time?' the woman asks him. He looks at her in bewilderment and says, 'I stepped on a duck.'"

A terrifying silence descended upon us. A moment later, peals of laughter tore it to shreds, and I heaved a breath of relief.

"It's a terrible joke," Nicole punted between the bouts of laughter. "So, so bad."

I agreed. So much in the human world hinged on a person's appearance which mattered little in where I came from.

"Yet you're laughing." I grinned with satisfaction.

"There is just something in the way you speak that sounds kind of...sweet." She paused her gaze on me."

The bubble of relief grew bigger in my chest.

Her eyes flicked between mine.

"What's your name?"

"Invi," I said. "It's short for Invidia."

"Invidia? What an unusual name. Where is it from?"

"Latin," I said, making her laugh again.

I could stay like this forever, trapped in the bubble of her laughter and the warm feeling that was spreading through my chest. The rest of the world seemed to have fallen away completely. The club with its noise and stench was gone.

Sadly, the sound of a glass placed on the table snapped me out of this sweet trance. Nicole's companion set her glass down, and I remembered I'd paid no attention to her all this time. I didn't even know her name, which was extremely rude of me.

"My apologies," I addressed her with a polite bow. "We haven't been introduced yet."

The blonde woman gave me a tight smile.

"There is no need for introductions. Now, if you excuse

me..." She got up from the table abruptly and headed toward the corridor with the sign *Washrooms* over it.

I didn't mourn her departure, eager to spend some time one on one with Nicole. Yet when I turned back to her again, the smile had left her face.

She leaned across the table to me.

"I hate to break it to you, Invi. But you don't have a chance here."

AVAILABLE NOW

If you wish to learn more about the evil goddess Ghata and her *bracks*, please read the books in the world of the River of Mists. You can start with Madame Tan's Freakshow trilogy, or with any book 1 of the duets set in that world.

Seven Horny Sins

Let Me Claim You
Let Me Win You
Let Me Feed You

The World of the River of Mists

Fantasy and Paranormal Romance

Dark Orcs of Helfallow

Agor

Demons (Complete Series)

Demon Mine

The Forgotten

Grand Master

The Last Unforgiven - Cursed

The Last Unforgiven - Freed

Stand Alone Novels

The Real Thing

To Love A Monster

Midnight Coven Author Group

Wicked Warlock (Cursed Coven)

Science-Fiction Romance

My Holiday Tails

Married to Krampus

My Tiny Giant

My Birthday Getaway

New Year, New Planet

Mail Order Mom

My Pumpkin

What Makes an Alien a Dad?

Dark Anomaly Trilogy

Gravity

Power

Explosion

Stand Alone Novels

Experiment

Enduring (Valos Of Sonhadra)

About the Author

Marina Simcoe likes to write love stories with human heroines and non-human heroes who just can't live without them. She firmly believes that our contemporary world could always use a little bit of the extraordinary.

She has lots of fun exploring how her out-of-this-world characters with their own beliefs, values, and aspirations fit into our every-day life.

She lives in Canada with her very own extraordinary hero, their three little offspring, and a cat who is definitely out of this world.

facebook.com/MarinaSimcoeAuthor

instagram.com/marinasimcoeauthor

bsky.app/profile/marinasimcoe.bsky.social

bookbub.com/profile/marina-simcoe

goodreads.com/MarinaSimcoe

amazon.com/author/marinasimcoe

patreon.com/MarinaSimcoe

www.ingramcontent.com/pod-product-compliance
Lightning Source LLC
Chambersburg PA
CBHW061347310726
48974CB00001B/241